"Chung-Cha belongs to Christ," Father ⌐ ⌐d. "Even if you destroy me, God will still ⌐⌐ ghter."

The agent chuckled.

"And what if I destro⌐

‖‖‖‖‖‖‖‖‖‖‖‖‖‖‖‖‖
D1483695

Praise for *The Beloved Daughter* by Alana Terry

Grace Awards, First Place
IndieFab Finalist, Religious Fiction
Women of Faith Writing Contest, Second Place
Book Club Network Book of the Month, First Place
Reader's Favorite Gold Medal, Christian Fiction

"...an engaging plot that reads like a story out of today's headlines..." ~ *Women of Faith Writing Contest*

"In this meticulously researched novel, Terry gives readers everything a good novel should have — a gripping story, an uplifting theme, encouragement in their own faith, and exquisite writing." ~ *Grace Awards Judges' Panel*

"The Beloved Daughter is a beautifully written story." ~ *Sarah Palmer, Liberty in North Korea*

There was silence for such a long time Kennedy wondered if there was a problem with Carl's antique cell phone. Finally, Rose asked, "And so what happens if you get pregnant, and you're too young to actually have a baby?"

Defying all laws of inertia, the acceleration of Kennedy's heart rate crashed to a halt like a car plowing into a brick wall. "What do you mean?"

"Like, what if you're too young but you still get pregnant?"

"How young?" Kennedy spoke both words clearly and slowly, as if rushing might drive the timid voice away for good.

"Like thirteen."

Praise for *Unplanned* by Alana Terry

"Deals with **one of the most difficult situations a pregnancy center could ever face**. The message is **powerful** and the story-telling **compelling**." ~ William Donovan, *Executive Director Anchorage Community Pregnancy Center*

"Alana Terry does an amazing job tackling a very **sensitive subject from the mother's perspective**." ~ Pamela McDonald, *Director Okanogan CareNet Pregnancy Center*

"**Thought-provoking** and intense ... Shows **different sides of the abortion argument**." ~ Sharee Stover, *Wordy Nerdy*

"Alana has a way of sharing the gospel **without being preachy**." ~ Phyllis Sather, *Purposeful Planning*

Simon exhaled as he stretched his arms. "I wish we didn't have to say good-bye." His voice was distant.

Hannah stared at the moon. She would never sit here beside him again in this garden. "There are no good-byes in the kingdom of heaven," she whispered, hoping her words carried the conviction her soul lacked.

Praise for *Torn Asunder*
by Alana Terry

"Filled with suffering, yet ultimately has a **resounding message of hope**." ~ Sarah Palmer, Liberty in North Korea

"Alana has a **great heart for the persecuted church** that comes out in her writing." ~ Jeff King, President of International Christian Concern

"Faith and love are tested beyond comprehension in this **beautifully written Christian novel**." ~ Kathryn Chastain Treat, Allergic to Life: My Battle for Survival, Courage, and Hope

"**Not your average love story** - wrapped in suspense, this story of faith will stop your heart as you hope and weep right along with the characters." ~ Nat Davis, Our Faith Renewed

"Torn Asunder is an **enthralling, heart-aching novel** that calls your heart to action." ~ Katie Edgar, KTs Life of Books

Note: The views of the characters in this novel do not necessarily reflect the views of the author, nor is their behavior necessarily condoned.

Out of North Korea
Copyright © 2018 Alana Terry
ISBN 978-1-941735-71-8
June, 2018

Cover design by Kristin Designs

www.alanaterry.com

Out of North Korea

a novel by Alana Terry

"The cowering prisoners will soon be set free; they will not die in their dungeon, nor will they lack bread."

Isaiah 51:14

CHAPTER 1

I'm an American, and I'm in trouble.

Big trouble.

I'm not talking about the kind of trouble you get in when your computer crashes the night before your dissertation is due. Or the trouble you get into with the relatives when you forget to call your granny on what has got to be her 115th birthday.

That's not the kind of trouble I'm in right now. I wish it were. Even from where I sit on the atheist/agnostic spectrum, I don't think it's too strong for me to say I wish to God it were that easy.

In fact, I could even go so far as to say I wish I were back in that Chinese jail.

Yeah. That's how serious this is.

I'm an American. I'm fixating on the words like some meditative mantra at an enlightenment class, but as my interrogator stares me down while I sit here in my boxers and my not-so-stylish pair of handcuffs, I don't think he cares all that much about what's written on my passport.

Nor does he care that the lies and the crimes I've been accused of may very well cost me my life.

All he cares about is one thing. Breaking me down until I confess to whatever it is they think I've done. Unfortunately, after my last experience in North Korea, I have a pretty solid idea about what that means.

I'm shivering in my boxers. This little hotel room/office/holding cell/whatever the heck this place is can't be a degree over fifty, and I haven't seen my clothes since last night.

"Do you know where you are, American?" my interrogator asks. He's got this sneer on his face that's so quintessentially villainous he could be accused of overacting if anyone ever got this on film. Except I'm not in a movie. No Navy SEAL team or debonair James Bond type is going to break in here and rush to my rescue.

In Hollywood, the Americans always make it out alive. In this case, I think my chances are about as good as the guy who played Jar Jar Binks winning an Oscar for his performance in *Star Wars*.

In other words, I'm doomed. The biggest question isn't whether or not I'm going to die. It's how much this man — and all the others like him — are going to torture me before someone finally pulls the plug. Or the trigger.

Or whatever it is they're going to do to me.

Now maybe you understand why I'd rather still be a prisoner in China.

The man leans down and thrusts a pen and paper onto the desk where I've been chained. "Start writing," he barks.

I'm about to tell him that penmanship while handcuffed isn't a skill most citizens practice in America regardless of how they might do it in North Korea, but with his scowling face and my sitting here shivering in my boxers, I'm not sure how well the delivery would pull off. So instead, like a good little schoolboy, I ask, "What do you want me to write about?" And all the while I'm thinking about if I'd rather be rescued by James Bond, Navy SEALs, or one of those femme fatale spy characters like Angelina Jolie in *Salt.*

Heck, I would even take the Avengers or Peter Parker in his Spidey suit if I thought it'd increase my chances of surviving.

My overacting villain trope continues to grimace. I get the feeling that he imagines himself quite the intimidating specimen. Adding to the melodrama, he refuses to clear his throat but growls out in a raspy voice, "Start off by telling us who you are and why you snuck into North Korea to spy on our great nation."

CHAPTER 2

About fifteen minutes later, my personal North Korean interrogator Happy Face storms back in. "You have your confession ready?"

My wrists are so chafed I could probably write an entire five-point essay in blood more easily than this.

"Going a little slowly," I grumble.

"What? What did you call me?"

My new best friend apparently is afflicted with a scorching case of Little Man Syndrome. Lucky me.

"I said I need more time to work on it." I over-enunciate every word, wondering if Korean culture has perfected the subtle art of sarcasm the way we have in the grand old US of A.

He snatches the paper from me. "What is this?" He squints at my scribbles.

"It's my confession." Admittedly, my handwriting's illegible even when I'm not handcuffed to my desk. *If you just let me have my smart phone, I could dictate my confession ...*

4

ALANA TERRY

"What does this say, American?" He shoves the paper into my face.

"Do you need me to read it to you?"

He pauses, as if considering. That answers my question about sarcasm. He lets out a scoff of sorts, which I can only take to mean that he's taking me up on my offer.

I glance up. "You really want me to read this? Out loud?" I can't remember the last time I've had to stand up and read an essay I've written. Okay, so technically I can't stand up right at the moment, but it feels just as awkward. You know that dream about showing up to school in nothing but your underwear? I'm basically living it out right now.

Officer Good-Cheer scowls at me in dead earnestness. Seeing as how I have very little left to lose, I read — or attempt to read — the start of my confession.

"You asked me to explain how I ended up in your sacred little kingdom called North Korea. Let me tell you. There I was in China, on a visa with the full permission of both the Chinese government and the US Embassy, when all of a sudden, some thugs came up from behind and grabbed me and my friend."

"Thugs?"

I blink at him. "Yeah. Thugs. You know, *Godfather*, *Gangs of New York*. Thugs."

5

He blinks again.

I let out my breath. "Bad guys," I finally translate for him, and he grunts something which I take to mean he wants me to continue.

"After about three nights in the Chinese jail," I read, "and after being repeatedly denied the opportunity to speak to anyone from the US Embassy" — I steal a peek at him to make sure he's following my big words — "I was given a pill, which I was told was headache medicine. I woke up here this morning with no clothes on except my boxers, and some *thug*" — here I admit to some slight on-the-fly rewording — "demanding to know what I'm doing in North Korea."

"Liar!" The man lunges for my paper, tears it out of my hand, and proceeds to rip it up into little shreds. His eyes glisten menacingly, and I keep waiting for a director to yell *cut* and tell him he's overdoing it.

"You are a bad prisoner."

He stares at me expectantly, and I wonder what he's waiting for. Does he think I'm about to cower with my tail between my legs or start bawling my eyes out because he called me something mean?

"For your punishment, you will stand in the corner and think about what you have done."

I raise my eyebrows, the universal sign for *seriously?* He

wants to me stand in the corner — in my boxers no less — and think about how bad I am? Is that what he's saying? Should I tell him that in America, nobody gets put in timeout after the age of four?

"What are you doing, American?" he demands. "Why do you not obey?"

I have no idea why *Lord of the Rings* pops into my head now of all times, but I find myself making my best Sean Aston as Samwise impression by saying, "Begging your pardon, but last time I checked, I was still chained to this desk."

I wonder if he's going to tell me what a bad prisoner I am again, and if he does, I'm ready with a real doozy of a comeback: *Oh yeah? Well I think you're a lousy guard. So there.*

He unlocks my cuffs, but not for long enough that I can stretch out this awful pain in my shoulder. Next thing I know I'm in the corner, my hands are cuffed behind my back, my nose pointed straight at the wall. My guard slams the door shut behind him, and in the silence, I've got all the time in the world to *think about what I've done.*

Like how I ended up here. I spent the summer between Seoul and China working on my documentary of North Korean refugees. Nothing illegal, nothing to warrant an arrest. I probably wasn't too popular with the government over there because I was actually telling the world about the way the Chinese persecute North Korean immigrants, sending them home to face torture and imprisonment if they're caught, but the last time I checked, my US passport still promised me the freedom of speech.

I wasn't terribly surprised or even all that worried when I got arrested in China. I mean, what was the worst they could do? Slap my wrist and send me home, right? Except they didn't send me home. They drugged me, and I woke up a prisoner of the North Koreans. I don't understand any of it, and I've got to find a way to get free.

Hear that, God? Are you listening?

Discounting the last few days since my arrest, I'm pretty sure I haven't said a single prayer since I graduated high school, but now I can hear my Grandma Lucy's voice almost as clearly as if she were a little miniature angel sitting on my shoulder, shining halo over her head and everything.

Bless him, Father God, and fill him with great boldness and courage to spread your news to the nations, and *yada, yada, yada.*

I've made my way up and down the atheist/agnostic spectrum starting on day one of my undergrad orientation until now. But it's still nice to know that somewhere I've got a little old granny lady praying for me. That woman is so annoying with her religious fervor that as soon as we're done talking on the phone I have to jump onto my favorite atheist Reddit forum to vent, but as much as I despise the fundamental bigotry she stands for, I adore that little white-haired lady.

And I hope God doesn't let me die before I get the chance to tell her that one more time.

CHAPTER 3

Here I am again at my desk, except by now I suppose Captain Sadist must not consider me a flight risk because even though my wrists are handcuffed together, I'm not shackled to the furniture anymore. Maybe I've progressed from being a *bad prisoner* to a *below-average prisoner*.

Do North Koreans give their captives time off for good behavior? I seriously doubt it.

I've been ordered to write my confession again, the real reason I crossed the border and sneaked into North Korea, which is what they tell me I've done. Last night, after standing in my little bad-boy corner for what felt like hours, I was allowed to sleep — still in nothing but my boxers — and now the sun's just coming up for the day.

The Real Reason I Crossed the Border into North Korea. I've been promised that once I pass my writing assignment, I'll be rewarded with some sort of breakfast. My first meal since I woke up here yesterday.

When I was a kid, school felt just like a prison. And

writing essays, that was torture. It wasn't until I joined the high school newspaper that I realized the truth. If I'm allowed to write exactly what I wanted to write, I adore it. Add in the photography skills I first learned at a summer community class, and my destiny as a photojournalist was sealed.

For years, that's what I've done. As a freelancer blessed with a ten-thousand-dollar camera and a few fortuitous connections from my grad-school days, I've set my own hours, deadlines, and assignments. Until digital technology finally surpassed my own learned skill, I developed my film by hand, but now I'm addicted to the tech. It's been years since I've used pen and paper. I do all of my writing by dictation, yes, even most of my emails. None of these wide-ruled sheets of notebook paper that transport me into traumatized flashbacks of sixth grade English class.

For many writers, there's absolutely nothing more intimidating than a blank page. I write my name in the top right-hand corner. I've even given my essay a working title. *How I Ended up in North Korea.*

Unfortunately, that's all I've got down so far. Either Mr. Chuckles doesn't know or doesn't care that someone captured me in China, drugged me, and brought me here. I have no memories whatsoever of my journey, and every once in a while I wonder if I've ended up as part of some kind of terrible social experiment. Maybe in a minute or two, a whole slew of American film students is going to come out from behind the woodwork, slap me on the back, and tell me what a good sport I've been. For all I know, I'm still in China and this whole North Korea act is a gimmick.

I start writing on the page. One of Grandma Lucy's favorite Bible verses says *If the Son sets you free, you will be free indeed*, and connected to that in my head is another one of her Scripture quotes: *The truth shall set you free.* Don't ask me where it's from. I haven't opened a Bible in a decade, even the one she gave me as a Christmas present a few years ago, but her words play in my mind nonetheless.

The truth shall set you free.

Except my oh-so-pleasant guard doesn't believe me when I tell him the truth, so here I am. Stuck.

The truth shall set me free?

Seeing as how — yet again — I have literally nothing to lose, I give a little shrug and start my essay once more. This time, I add a subtitle.

My summer vacation in a North Korean jail.

Hey, my name's Ian McCallister. Did I mention yet that I'm an American? Got my passport somewhere. Maybe if you let me have my pants back I can dig through the pockets and show you.

12

You guys want to know what I'm doing in your blessed country of North Korea. Sure. I can answer that one. And just in case you're worried that I'm making stuff up, I'll even voluntarily put myself under oath. I, Ian McCallister, a resident of Cambridge, Massachusetts, do hereby swear that I am in my own right mind and under no compulsion — save for the handcuffs around my wrists — to tell the truth, the whole truth, and nothing but the truth, so help me God.

Except I'm pretty sure you guys are supposed to be even greater atheists than I am, so that leaves us in a kind of bind, doesn't it? I could swear on your Dear Leader or something like that, but I'm not sure how happy that'd make your higher-ups.

This is my essay on what I did over summer vacation in North Korea.

I got drugged. I woke up. And here I was.

What I've learned from this big mistake is to never take candy from a stranger, and always bring a buddy with you to the club so you can keep an eye on each other's drinks.

I would like to apologize to the North Korean government for any hassle my unwilling abduction may have caused and hereby formally and with all due respect request that as a punishment for my crimes, I get sent back to my home in the United States ASAP. I also would hate to think that I might be leaving any incendiary or revolutionary materials behind to corrupt your impressionable masses. Therefore, I humbly request that my laptop, camera, and all other recording information suffer the same fate as I will.

Respectfully yours,

Ian (who I hope is no longer on your naughty list)

CHAPTER 4

Lessons learned from my first two days in North Korea:

1) Officer Grumpy doesn't have much of a sense of humor.

2) Neither do any of the other guards here.

I've been standing in the corner since breakfast. Guy Smiley wasn't too impressed with my second attempt at a report, either. I swear, that man's more difficult to write for than my sophomore year journalism professor. She hated me because I happen to be a white male (if you hadn't noticed), and unfortunately I never got the memo warning guys like me to stay away from her class. This guy here at the jail, I don't know what his deal is. But I'm back in the corner.

Again.

Good news though.

Turns out I must have totally cut off blood supply to my nerves or something because my shoulders don't feel a thing. I've got to tell my chiropractor back in the States about this.

Persistent shoulder pain? Try standing with your hands cuffed behind your back for a few hours! If she ever publishes that in a professional journal, I'm going to make sure she cites me as her main source.

Sun's about to go down. I'm keeping my mind alert by trying to figure out what time it must be in Washington, back where Grandma Lucy is praying for me. Because there's only one thing that woman loves just as much as her talk-with-Jesus times, and that's her afternoon nap. So I figure that there's going to be an hour at some point in what ends up being my early morning where she's settling down for her nap the day before (three cheers for the International Date Line), and that's the one hour of the day I'm going to allow myself to freak out. Other than that, it's all good.

What about when Grandma Lucy sleeps at night, you might wonder? Well, don't worry about that. She always jokes that she sleeps like a baby. By which she means she wakes up every couple hours, prays in bed, and goes back for another little snooze. And seriously, I've even heard her praying in her sleep. You might think I'm joking, but I'm not.

So I'm covered.

Literally (if you're the kind of person who likes the idea of prayers actually covering you).

And agnostic as I am — you've heard the saying, I'm sure, that we gingers lack souls — still the thought makes me feel pretty good.

It's still at least ten hours or more before morning, before that tiny bit of my day that I've allotted for freaking out. So I have to pace myself until then. Sometimes I start to worry about all the terrible things they might do to me (you know, like if they decide it's time to put an end to the corner-standing and instead force me into a dunce hat or something). I'm distracting myself by thinking of what I'll write about my time here. I just wish I had my camera too so I could record everything I've seen. When I'm not imagining the exact angle I'd use to get the right shot, I come up with names for the chapters of my unwritten memoir.

Listen to this. The ridiculous write-out-my-confessions-as-an-essay thing? I'm going to call it *And I Thought Sixth Grade was a Pain in the Butt.*

And then I figure I can do a whole chapter about the handcuffs. I'm thinking of something with a little double entendre because, you know. Handcuffs. Or if that's too risqué, I could simply call it *With Apologies to my Chiropractor.*

So far, there hasn't been any sign of torture devices, but isn't that the first thing most people will think of when they hear there's an American imprisoned in North Korea? So if the punishment does happen to fall into the cruel and unusual category and I live to tell about it in my New York Times bestselling exposé memoir, I'll call that chapter *Why I'll Never Go to the Dentist Again.*

Other than that, I'm working my way up toward Compliant Prisoner instead of Naughty Boy in the Corner. I really am trying to decide what I'm supposed to say because we all know what's going to happen next. Old Principal Jailer's going to march in here, order me in that chair again, shove his college-ruled notebook paper in front of me, and expect me to write out my five-hundred words in #2 pencil.

It's already become pretty clear he wants something besides the truth. If only I can figure out what that is, we can get past this purgatory stage. Yes, I'm making a Catholic reference. *Forgive me, Grandma Lucy, for I have sinned ...*

No, that one wouldn't go over well with her either.

But I have decided that purgatory is exactly where I am. Think about it. Take everything you know about this place, including the very few stories of Americans like me who have been fortunate enough to be invited to see the insides of the North Korean justice system, and picture what you think my biggest worries should be.

We're talking torture, hard labor, starvation, the works,

right? Let's just go ahead and say it. Not like I can get even more freaked out, you know. So, since I was taught from my earliest days as a journalism student not to mince words, let's just call it what it is.

Hell.

If they prosecute me here, it's going to be hell.

The other option is they'll decide they've made some horrible, terrible mistake, and they'll fly me back to America with a box of chocolates to pass along to the Secretary of State with their heartfelt apologies for this little international misunderstanding. And as disgruntled as I may be with the current administration, standing in front of Secretary Hamilton and offering her Pyongyang's finest delicacies (preferably after I've had a chance to take a scalding hot shower and change out of these stupid boxers) is about as close to heaven as a man in my situation can hope for right about now.

So — not to insult your intelligence but to carry my metaphor out to its final destination — hopefully by now it's crystal clear why I chose to call my current situation purgatory. I'm not sure if it's supposed to be capitalized because it's the name of a place. Hmm. Wonder what the Chicago Manual would have to say about that. Good thing by the time it comes to write my New York Times bestseller

I'll have a publisher and a slew of editors to look up that stuff on my behalf.

I don't know a ton about Catholicism. If you were to talk to most of the folks at Grandma Lucy's church, being Catholic is about as serious a crime as being — cue gasps and involuntary shudders — a liberal. But somewhere in the back of my head is this idea that purgatory's quicker for some people than others. And I know that if I were in your shoes and was listening to me whine, I'd be thinking, *Wow, at least he's not getting tortured or anything. That lucky dog should hope he stays so fortunate.*

But now that I'm here, standing in the corner with nothing to do but fear the unknown and try to hold off my panic attack until sometime tomorrow morning, I have to wonder if that's all wrong. What if the psychological torment of uncertainty, the fear of torture, is just as bad or even worse than the suffering itself?

In other words, what if purgatory really is nothing but a different kind of hell?

On that happy note, I adjust my weight and try to stretch my shoulders (did I mention they're completely numb?), and a staticky voice from some speaker barks at me in Korean what I assume either means *hold still and stop fidgeting* or *your mama's so fat her belt size is the equator.* Not quite sure. I've never been all that great with languages other than my own.

I think about studies way back from my Psych 101 days, how a dog would rather be beaten than neglected. (Don't ask me how any publication could get away with citing a research project like that. I didn't take my first ethics class until I was a junior.) The point of the morally questionable study was simple enough for a first-year to grasp: Even torture is better than solitary confinement.

I adjust my legs one more time and smile slightly at the wall when my radio friend yells at me again. The next time I'm preparing for imprisonment inside of North Korea I'll have to ask someone to teach me a few Korean jokes so I can interact better with my captors.

For now, the radio yelling means I'm not totally alone after all.

And I hate to admit how twisted it sounds, but that's comforting to know at a time and place like this.

CHAPTER 5

Well, it's official. I hate writing assignments. Guess that means I made the right call so many years ago when I decided to go freelance. Unfortunately my cheerful, benevolent captor is making me rewrite my confession. Again.

Oh, joy.

I've come to find out he actually has a name, by the way — the guard assigned to me, I mean, not my essay. And I know this is going to come to you as quite a shock, with me being stuck here in Korea and all, but at least his name — now that I know it — is easy to remember. You ready for this?

Officer Kim.

Original, isn't it?

I can just hear the conversation I'm going to have with my editor now.

"You can't name the guard Officer Kim. It's far too derivative. Some would call it downright racist."

"But that's his name."

"Well, we've got to change it."

"But that's his name."

"Do you want to become the number one New York Times bestseller or not?"

I pause for a minute to think then finally ask, "How does Mr. Grumpy sound? Is that any better?"

"What was his given name? Maybe we can use that."

"Hee-Man."

"I beg your pardon?"

"His name is Hee-Man."

"You're joking with me. Hee-Man Kim?"

"No. Kim Hee-Man. They put the family name first in Asia."

Turns out you can have all kinds of interesting conversations when you're forced to stand in a corner for hours on end.

But Hee-Man — fine, I'm using his given name to preemptively appease my imaginary future editor — has added a few other punishments to my daily regimen. Maybe he's worried that I'm not getting enough physical activity standing in the corner. It's thoughtful of him to be looking out for my health like that, don't you think? So in addition to the fire in my neck that's going to take at least a few dozen chiropractic adjustments to work out, my thighs are burning up because Hee-Man has been forcing me to do wall squats.

"Wall squats?" I can hear my future editor ask.

"Yes. Wall squats. It's where you have to stand with your legs bent at a ninety-degree angle with your back against the wall until …"

"I know what they are. But don't you think it's a little far-fetched? I mean, you realize that you're a prisoner in North Korea. Readers are going to expect to hear about you getting beaten with rods or injected with hallucinogens, starved half to death, that kind of thing."

"Oh, they starved me all right. But they also made me do wall squats. By the way, does your publishing company offer retroactive worker's comp? Can I give you my chiropractor bill?"

"Wait a minute. Hold up. You said they starved you. So why are we focusing on the wall squats? Let's talk about the starvation. You've only got a few pages to hook readers. You've got to grab them right from the beginning. Nobody wants to hear about an American prisoner being forced to do calisthenics. They want the anguish, the ennui. Picture yourself back in that prison room. What thoughts are going through your brain? How do you feel?"

"Hungry."

"Give me more. What hurts right now? What's causing you pain?"

"My shoulders. Didn't I say that already?"

She rolls her eyes at me. "I mean emotional pain."

"Oh." I pause to think. "I miss my girlfriend."

Her expression lights up. "A girlfriend? Great. We can lead with that. How long have you been together? How serious is the relationship?"

I shrug. "She broke up with me right before I got arrested."

She raises her eyebrow. "So you're not even together anymore?"

Another shrug. "It's complicated."

A prolonged sigh. "Okay, let's ditch the girlfriend angle. But we need to give the reader your experiences, let them walk around some in your shoes."

"I didn't have any shoes. I woke up in nothing but my boxers."

"Forget the boxers. Let's focus on your emotional state. Which reminds me, PTSD is all the rage now. Do you have flashbacks? Maybe uncontrollable urges to just punch someone?"

"I'm getting one of those urges right now."

"Smart aleck. You should have stuck with freelance."

"My sentiments exactly."

It's my fourth day here, which, if you count the three days I spent in a Chinese jail before they drugged me and whisked me over the border, means I've been without my freedom for a full week. I'm not joking about the starving part either. Not really. Officer Kim, a.k.a. Hee-Man (you're welcome, Mr. or Ms. Literary Agent), comes in every morning to eat his breakfast in front of me. He assures me that if I write out my full confession, I can have some too, but it's usually not until the middle of the day when he comes in and begrudgingly hands me a few spoonfuls of rice. If I'm really lucky, he will have thought to add a couple limp vegetables on top. I could literally finish the meal off in two bites. Usually I do, no matter how often I promise myself I'm going to ration.

I've been thinking about that movie *Martian* quite a bit. Good old American boy, a.k.a. Matt Damon (who really remembers the name of the character if he's being played by Matt Damon?), has to find a way to survive on Mars completely by himself. Did you know that the book it's based on was written by an indie author? And look how it took off. With all the fights I have in my head with my future literary editor, I sometimes wonder if I should go the self-publishing route when it comes time to write my memoirs.

Problem is I can't write my stinking memoir until I'm out of this prison, and Hee-Man has made it very clear I'm not coming out of this prison until I've written a confession that's up to his standards. He wants to know how I got into North Korea, who sent me, and what mission directives I was given by the US government. He wants the names of all the officials involved in my so-called espionage.

We've gone around in enough circles for me to realize that Hee-Man's not looking for the real story. No matter how many times I tell him about that "Tylenol" I took in China, he's not going to believe me. And I'm sick of writing the exact same thing over and over.

No room for originality or creative expression.

So today I'm going to have a little fun. I've already told Hee-Man that I'm ready to set the record straight, that the whole thing about my getting arrested in China was a lie and a hoax, and if he brings me extra paper today, I'll tell him the full story.

It's a win-win as far as I see it. I get to write something different than my summer vacation getting drugged in China. And he gets to read something far more interesting than the drivel I've given him over the past few days.

Once I start scribbling, the words flow. It's the author's elusive dream, the coveted writer's high. Sometimes I catch myself laughing out loud before I remember that this is supposed to be serious. I hope that when all is said and done, Hee-Man lets me keep these notebook pages because I know my girlfriend will laugh her head off when she reads it.

I have no idea how long it takes me to finish. It might be hours. My body's surging with adrenaline, my mood is lighter than it's been all week, and finally I write those two words that are every author's greatest dream:

The end.

"Ready," I call out, certain that every word and action is being monitored in real time. Sure enough, Hee-Man saunters in and smiles when he sees how many pages I'm holding out for him.

"Good." He nods his head. "That is very good. I am glad you decided to cooperate."

I don't say anything and only smirk as he takes the stack of papers away. I don't know how much trouble I'm going to get into for what I just wrote, but I replay some of the best one-liners I put in there and allow myself a metaphorical pat on the back.

I've always known it's going to be my humor that gets me through whatever fate has in store for me. There's not a whole lot I wouldn't give to watch Hee-Man's reaction as he reads my so-called confession.

CHAPTER 6

My friendly neighborhood interrogator is back after only ten or fifteen minutes. I have no idea what to expect. Maybe he'll be so sick of me and my snarky personality, he'll decide it's time to move me up from preschool punishment tactics and let the real torture finally begin. What I'm hoping for is that after reading my essay, Hee-Man will be so sick of my antics that he'll decide I'm no longer worth his time and order me back across the border to China, never to return to his great nation of North Korea again.

Fine by me, old chap.

What I'm not prepared for is for Hee-Man to walk in here, sit down at the desk across from me, and tell me in all earnestness, "These are quite serious allegations you bring against yourself, American."

I stare at him. "What?"

He sighs. "Very serious." Next thing I know, he's clucking his tongue at me. I suppose this is the part where I'll get lectured about not taking my situation seriously

29

enough. The part where I'm handed yet another stack of notebook paper and told to start over, this time with the truth.

Only that's not what happens.

"Just a few questions before I pass this on to my superiors."

I don't know if it's because I'm eating less than two-hundred calories a day, but I find myself unable to do anything but stare at him. It's like a bad comedy sketch.

"First question." Hee-Man's tone is all official as he straightens up the notebook pages full of my scribbles. "This Fury character. Is he with the CIA?"

Blink.

"All right then. If you refuse to answer that, I want you to tell me about your girlfriend. Natasha Romanoff, is it? She is working on your side now, so may we assume that she has cut ties with Russia?"

Blink. All of a sudden, I wonder if my ingenious streak of hilarity is going to be what brings the guillotine down on my neck instead of what gets me out of here.

"You are not being very helpful, American. I have many other questions too. What is this secret serum the American army is using to enhance the performance of its soldiers? How many others are there like this" — he glances down at my page — "Captain America, as you call him?"

It's too much for me. "It's a joke, dude."

Now it's Hee-Man's turn to be the one to blink.

"Joke," I repeat. "Marvel? *The Avengers?*"

I get nothing from him.

"Hollywood?" I try.

His eyes light up in recognition. "Now I see. We always suspected that your American intelligence agency used movies to spread not only Western propaganda but secret messages to our enemies. Tell me, which organization is behind all this?"

I can't believe it. "Give me that." I try to yank the notebook pages out of his hands, wanting nothing more than to tear them up. It was my finest work, at least in the past week, but suddenly I'm not feeling in such a grandiose mood.

"It was a joke," I repeat. "You guys do joke on this half of the peninsula, don't you?"

Hee-Man holds my paper and flicks a speck of invisible dust from off the shoulder of his uniform. "Mr. McAllister, I understand that in America they do things differently. But I want to assure you that if you had any idea of the allegations being brought against you even as we speak, you would recognize in an instant that your situation is far from humorous."

He stands up and walks out, apparently so upset he doesn't remember to force me into the corner to think about what I've done.

CHAPTER 7

The sun has just gone down when Hee-Man returns. It's been a relatively easy day since I pulled that Avengers stunt. If I would have known that the biggest danger I'd face while trapped in a North Korean prison was boredom, I would have brought my tablet and gotten caught up on some Netflix.

"Get up. It is time to go," Hee-Man tells me. I have no way to tell if he's angrier than normal. To me he looks just as grumpy, but no more so than usual. Still, I feel a slight ripple of excitement. I haven't left this room in four days. Right now, I'm more concerned about the chance to stretch my legs than I am curious or worried about where he might be leading me.

Even though Hee-Man never ordered me in the corner this morning, I've decided it's not worth risking my neck anymore. I learned nothing in school if not that people in authority rarely have patience with smart alecks. I get up and follow Hee-Man with a puppy-like obedience that would make the skulking Sméagol himself proud.

32

"In here." Hee-Man gestures, and I'm disappointed that my first outing as a so-called guest of the North Korean government is only down the hall. Still, it's enough that I pick up on a few new facts I hadn't known before.

One: I don't think this is an actual jail, handcuffs, guards, and interrogation sessions notwithstanding. It feels more like a dorm room or some kind of deserted hotel.

Only not quite as deserted as I suspected. Which brings me to point two: Hee-Man and I aren't the only ones here. Of course, I had my suspicions. If Hee-Man had to keep watch 24-7, he'd never get the chance to use the bathroom, let alone sleep. I pass a room with a small window in the door, and I count at least three other officers in the same olive green uniforms as my friend. They don't look at me — which is just as well seeing as how I'm still in my undies — but it means Hee-Man and I aren't alone.

I tuck this information away, knowing full well that I'll have plenty of time to digest it later when I'm doing wall squats or standing in the corner to atone for some petty sin or other. Right now I follow Hee-Man into a small closet of a room. On a table in the corner sits a laptop that's literally being held together by duct tape.

"Take a seat."

Something's changed in Hee-Man's tone, which is

striking to note, given that his voice is just as expressionless as always. I detect the subtle difference nonetheless, even if I can't pinpoint a reason for the shift.

"I want you to tell me what this is." He leans over and clicks the mouse. The picture takes nearly a full minute to load, but I know exactly what it is after just seeing the top sliver.

"You recognize this photograph?" Hee-Man asks once it's fully revealed on the screen.

No more bravado. No more jokes. "Yes."

"Will you tell me about it?"

I take in a deep breath, surprised I'm able to find my voice. "This is a picture I took several years ago."

I stare, completely unable to blink. There's something of a legend in the photojournalist world. That one elusive shot. The one chance you have to snap a photo that changes your entire career. For Dorothea Lange, it was the mother sitting on the porch with her children, the epitome of the suffering and poverty that marked the American Great Depression. In the international journalism world, you've got your image of the young Afghan refugee with her striking blue eyes, the little naked girl running through a Vietnam field after a napalm attack.

Every good photojournalist — or so the legend goes —

gets their one shot at a picture like this. If you're ready, if you've done your homework, and if you're extremely lucky, you end up with a photograph that not only launches your career but can incite public sympathy, enact policy change, and yes — as naïve and trite as it sounds — change the world.

Two thoughts run through my head at once. *Man, I'm good.* And *I wish my girlfriend were here to see this.*

"We have been doing our research on you," Hee-Man tells me. "This is not your first time coming to our country."

"No." It's not that I'm being intentionally vague, cryptic, or untalkative. It's just that I've dreamed about this photograph, literally seen it in my sleep, but even my subconscious mind was unable to project how striking it would turn out.

I guess I really am that good.

Hee-Man lets out a heavy sigh. "Tell me about your first trip to North Korea." At first, I'm afraid he's going to hand me another stack of notebook paper, but then he pulls out a tape recorder.

Yes, that's what I said. A tape recorder. Not a smart phone. Not a wireless mic. It's like I'm living with my grandma in the pre-Internet days all over again.

Hee-Man presses record, and I watch the wheels of the

cassette tape start to turn, accompanied by a low whirring. He rattles off a few things in Korean, but all I catch is my name, and then he sets the recorder closer to me and says, "Now, tell us everything you know about this photograph."

CHAPTER 8

I don't leave anything out.

It was my first trip here, the only time I voluntarily entered this country. Everything was perfectly legit. Through a travel agency, I managed to get my hands on a tourist visa, and I flew to North Korea. The countryside was still reeling after the devastating floods and subsequent famine from a few years earlier, and I'd been told not to expect to travel anywhere outside of Pyongyang. Even then, wherever our tour group went, we had two minders assigned to us. Think tour guide, chaperone, spy, and babysitter all wrapped up into one role. That's what the minders did. The reason there were two? Easy. So they could keep an eye on each other as well as on us foreigners.

The first few days of my trip were very rote. Proud visits to shopping malls that lacked nothing except customers and cash registers. Ostentatiously decorated hotel lobbies with a full staff and no guests. We even saw a grocery store where all the boxes and cans of food on display were empty decoys. And yet this is what our tour guides/babysitters showed us, convinced we'd accept it as proof of North Korea's prosperity.

Some people I talked to after my return from Pyongyang were surprised that I got in at all. Why would a nation so backwards and closed off allow any visitors in? The answer has more to do with internal politics than anything else. In the same way that the fake stores and businesses were on constant display, our small group was also on show, a prop meant to convince the average North Korean that their country truly was the greatest on earth.

See? Even foreigners long for the honor of visiting our great nation so they can experience the utopia our leaders have built.

It was all very formal and scripted, the entire visit. One of the minders, the younger of the pair, was curious enough to ask me a few questions about America, but his partner discouraged any one-on-one conversation, so we rarely found the opportunity to speak freely.

Everything changed on the second to last day of our trip. Our minder announced that we'd been granted special permission to take a bus north to see some of the rural landscape. Like I already said, everything about our visit was staged, including what photographs we were allowed to take, but the countryside was beautiful in the early spring. Both minders, perhaps tired by the end of their busy week following us around, grew more lax, and I managed to slip away from the group and do some wandering on my own.

That's when I found him. Even though I never saw my photograph until today, that boy's face has remained permanently seared into my memory. Sunken, hollow cheeks. Shoulder blades and clavicle protruding out from beneath his tattered shirt. Mud caked onto his entire body while he squatted in the dirt, foraging for food.

This was it. My one chance. I had to act. The minders would catch up with me at any moment. I grabbed the shot in the same instant that the boy noticed me. His eyes locked onto mine. Haunted. He couldn't be any more than six or seven, but his eyes looked a century old.

Snap. He jumped up and ran away. I'd been so obsessed about getting the shot, so pumped full of adrenaline at having this life-changing encounter dropped into my lap, that I didn't even think to wonder how scared I must have made him. He'd probably never seen an American before, or someone with hair as red as mine. It was possible he didn't even know what a camera was.

I felt bad. I hadn't meant to ruin his foraging, but I had bigger things to worry about when I heard my minders running up the path toward me.

I knew not to press my luck, no matter how perfect the timing of that shot was, no matter what kind of reception it could have elicited if I were to take it back home. My film had just run out. Before the minders could reach me, I yanked it out, tossed it into its canister, and tossed it beneath a bush. I knew they would question me, but I hoped that if I showed them my empty camera, they'd forget about it, and if I was lucky, I could come back to hunt for the film later.

I suppose at the time I underestimated just how desperately Pyongyang wanted to keep up appearances in the international media. According to official reports from within North Korea, the famine never even happened. Children in their great nation were healthy and chubby and full of life. There was no way they'd allow me to take home evidence proving their statements were lies.

Knowing what I know now about North Korea, having heard a few other stories of foreigners arrested here, I got off fairly lucky that time. Sure, there were lectures. Plenty of lectures. Lectures from both my minders together and next from one then the other separately. Lectures from the local police, who my minders decided to get involved. By then, I was sure I'd never recover that film, and I was never let out of my minders' sight until I boarded the airplane the next day with strict warnings that I was never allowed to return to their country.

I can't explain how many hours of sleep I've lost thinking about the picture of that little homeless boy. If I had been allowed to take it back to the States, my life would been thrust onto an entirely different trajectory. I wouldn't have to strive to carve out my name alongside staff photojournalists backed up by all the big-name publications. There would be awards. Grandma Lucy would preach a hefty sermon at me about the evil and folly of pride, but in my opinion, false humility is just as grave of a sin. As I stare at this photograph, I know that I'm staring at what could have gone down as the image of the decade. No, I'll go even farther. I may have taken the shot of the century.

But what did it cost me?

Up until now, I couldn't figure out why the North Koreans were interrogating me or why the Chinese would drag me here over the border in the first place, but the pieces are starting to come together.

Somehow, Pyongyang got their hands on my film. Whoever handled it knew what they were doing, and I begrudgingly admit that there's not a whole lot I would have done differently if I had developed the image myself. I'm sure in their heads, this photograph makes me some sort of

41

subversive Western enemy who planned to use this image to incite foreign nations to conspire to overthrow their government. China and North Korea have been in bed together for decades. It's such common knowledge, neither country even tries to hide it, so I can only assume that someone somewhere in China figured I'd be worth a lot to the North Koreans if they handed me over.

I wonder if I'm supposed to feel flattered.

Any sane man would be shaking in his boxers.

But all I can do is stare straight into the eyes of this little starving child and wonder how both our lives might have changed if I'd managed to get his picture home.

CHAPTER 9

Hee-Man's expression is just as indecipherable as ever when he asks me, "Who is this Pit Sir you mentioned?"

"Pul-it-zer," I respond, dragging out each syllable. "It's an award for journalists. A very important award."

Hee-Man scratches his beardless chin. "So you planned to use this award to overthrow our government?"

I sigh, not caring if my frustration is showing. "It has nothing to do with your government." Can't he see that by now? "Honestly and truly, this is all about me. My ambition. Me standing up and accepting that award, getting my name written down in the history books. That's all."

Is Hee-Man so caught up in his conformist upbringing that he truly has no notion of selfish ambition? "So you are saying it was not your government who told you to take this picture and smuggle it back to your Western newspapers?"

Maybe he's finally starting to understand. Dare I hope? "That's exactly what I'm saying." In fact, it's what I've been saying for the past half hour. We're still in the same room as before, only I've asked him to turn off that computer. As proud as I might be in any other circumstance to see how perfectly my photo turned out, it's too distracting right now. Too disappointing. My only hope is that I can finally get it into Hee-Man's head that my photograph of the starving little boy was an attempt to further my own career. Once he realizes I have nothing to do with the CIA, the American military, or the Marvel Avengers, he'll have no choice but to let me go.

Right?

In the name of full disclosure, I know that I'm not being fully honest with Hee-Man as I go on and on about how this photograph is all about me and my acclaim. Sure, who wouldn't want "Pulitzer Prize winner" included right beneath their byline? But as selfish and ambitious as I may be, I do what I do because I believe in the power of journalism to make a difference in this dark and miserable place we call earth. I believe that the right photograph taken at the right time can sway public opinion more than any other kind of media. Do I want to see the children of North Korea fed and educated and clothed and properly cared for? Absolutely.

Do I think this photograph could have gone miles to rallying people in the free world to work toward that end?

I do. But that certainly doesn't mean I was sent here as a spy, and it certainly doesn't mean I have actual plans to overthrow the Pyongyang government, plans that somehow start with me smuggling this image out of North Korea and sharing it with the Western world.

I think Hee-Man is starting to realize that too. At least I hope so. Hard as it is to admit, he's my only connection right now, either with Pyongyang or anybody on the outside. If I can get him to believe me, I'm one step closer to getting home.

I've never been more ready to find myself back in the United States.

CHAPTER 10

"So you're telling me I'm getting out of here?" My throat nearly catches at the words. I suppose a full week of being starved and interrogated can do that to even the strongest of psyches.

Hee-Man smiles genuinely at me. "Yes, I will escort you myself to Pyongyang, and from there it's just a few formalities."

"What sort of formalities?" I ask. I don't even care about the details. I can't believe I'm on my way out of here.

"You will be made to sign a confession. Very simple."

"And then I'll be released?"

"I should say so."

I'm so ecstatic I could hug him. I wonder how much Hee-Man had to do with advocating for my release. Was it our conversation about that photograph that changed his mind? Did I manage to successfully convince him I'm nothing but an arrogant and ambitious journalist, not a subversive spy?

I get the feeling that my life and my freedom are eternally

indebted to this man, and I mentally apologize for all the horrid nicknames I gave him during my first few days imprisoned here.

"How long of a trip is it to Pyongyang?" I ask. He doesn't answer. I don't give him time to. "How long will all the paperwork take? Do you think they'll send me home tonight?"

I'm certain Hee-Man can't be a full decade older than I am, but his smile is paternal. He pats me on the shoulder. "Stop your worrying, American. All the arrangements have been taken care of. Just be patient, and you will be home in no time at all."

Home. The word swells in my chest as soon as I hear it. I wonder if they've already let Grandma Lucy know I'm going to be released. I hope so. She's so old and frail, I've been worried that the stress of having a grandson in jail might give her another heart attack.

I usually return to Washington once a year as part of my obligatory December pilgrimage, but I'm already planning to spend my first week or two of freedom there. Let Aunt Connie spoil me with her home-baked cinnamon rolls and cookies. I'll even listen to Grandma Lucy's extended prayer sessions and sermons. There are so many people I want to get in touch with. People I'm sure have been worried about me. I don't know if my cell phone is here or still in China, but there are at least a dozen people I want to call, not the least of which is my girlfriend.

Who's technically now my ex-girlfriend.

I may have mentioned earlier that it's complicated.

I'm so dizzy at the word *home* I'm already jumping into New Year's resolution mode, even though it's only the end of summer. So many things I've promised myself not to take for granted anymore. Family. Friendships.

I've only been half aware that I've been doing it, but this whole week stuck here with Hee-Man, I've been making bargains with God. I'm sure you know exactly what I mean. *God, if you only get me out of here, I'll start going to church again. I'll commit my life to justice and charitable works if you only set me free.*

Well, I still don't believe that there's necessarily some sentient being up there overseeing my future and securing my freedom, but I certainly do believe in karma, and the universe has just done me a solid. I doubt a lifetime of selflessness and good deeds is going to make a dent on my tab, but I'm sure looking forward to trying.

These are all the thoughts going through my head as Hee-Man hands me my clothes and leads me to a bathroom stall where he says I can take a shower.

ALANA TERRY

A shower. Who would have thought something so simple could be this luxurious?

I'm overflowing with gratitude. I'm making vows to get along better with others, to focus more on using my gifts to shed light on injustice instead of trying to advance my own career. I'm going to consume less and recycle more and let Grandma Lucy and everyone else in my family know how much I love them. I've also resolved to take my cues from Ben Affleck in *Good Will Hunting*, because once I get out of here, I've got to go see about a girl.

And once I tell her how I feel, I'm never going to take my freedom for granted again.

I recite my resolutions as I stand under the shower, rejoicing in the tepid water that symbolically washes away the dirt and the stress and the fear of this past week.

I'm going home.

And not a moment too soon.

CHAPTER 11

It's like Hee-Man is my brand-new best friend, like we've been separated since elementary school and only now are getting the chance to catch up on one another's lives. While the driver speeds — and by speeds I'm talking about 35 mph — toward Pyongyang, Hee-Man sits with me in the backseat and asks about everything from my favorite foods to my love life.

"You have a wife in America?"

I shake my head.

"Girlfriend?"

This is answered with a shrug. "Sort of." It's a long story, and I don't think he really wants to hear all about how I got dumped just before my arrest, but after enough prying even that comes out.

"So she will not date you because you are not of the same religion?"

I nod. "Pretty much sums it up." Hey, if millions of lives are lost in wars fueled by religious differences, who am I to be surprised when a romance is called off for the same?

Even a romance as beautiful and close as our own?

I decide to change the subject. "What about you? Do you have a family?" I know from my last experience with my North Korean minders that Hee-Man probably isn't expected to tell me much about his personal life, so I'm surprised when he starts talking about his wife and two little girls. When we get to the subject of his oldest starting kindergarten, he wants to know what the education system is like in America. I've got plenty to say on the matter, or plenty I could say. The one documentary I managed to sell to the networks was about a school system in Detroit where underprivileged kids were being forced into a building built on toxic land. It was a perfect example of nearly everything that's wrong with the American educational system: overcrowded classrooms, school boards who care far more about lining their own pockets than they do about their children's health or safety, and rampant inequality that automatically favors the privileged children whose parents have the time, political empowerment, and language skills necessary to advocate for their children.

I decide it's best to not mention any of this to my friend, however, so I make a few blanket statements that could be taken straight out of the Presidential State of the Union address.

Hee-Man shakes his head sadly. "I feel sorry for the children in America," he exclaims, his voice full of sympathy. "They probably do not even realize they are being brainwashed, do they?"

I keep my mouth shut, and we drive along this stretch of bumpy rural road — apparently a highway by North Korean standards — in silence.

"Do you want to listen to some music?" Hee-Man finally asks.

I've seen pictures of North Korean schoolchildren playing kid-sized accordions, and that's the image that flits into my head. I shrug and answer, "Sure."

Hee-Man tells the driver something in Korean, and soon I'm listening to a haunting ballad. The woman's voice is low and sultry, which surprises me even though I can't say why. I feel like I'm listening to something that could have been played as the last slow song at my high-school prom. Except it's in a foreign language. Hee-Man is swaying softly in time with the music, his shoulder gently bumping mine every second and fourth beat.

I have no idea what the words are, but I guess they're telling the truth when they say that music is the universal language. It's obviously a love song, and if there were ever a Korean version of the *Titanic* movie, I'm convinced this is what they would play during the closing credits.

Hee-Man bumps into me a little more enthusiastically. "Do you like it?"

I'm surprised when he begins to sing along, his voice a high tenor to match the woman's low alto. There is a passion in the music and a tenderness in Hee-Man's face that compels me to ask, "What is it about?"

He stopped swaying, and I worry that I've upset him by interrupting his karaoke.

"What do you mean?"

"The song," I answered. "What's she singing about?"

He stares at me blankly.

"The words," I finally explain. What are the words?"

Hee-Man nods in understanding, listens for a moment, and begins to translate.

"*He loved us with eternal love. He gave his life for our good. I sing his praise, I tell of his greatness. I expectedly wait until the day we meet again.*"

I'm certain something must have gotten lost in translation because the lyrics remind me of the hymns they sing at Grandma Lucy's old-fashioned country church. Not what you'd listen to on the pop station in Korea.

Hee-Man looks over at me, and there's a glint in his eye. I can't tell if it's from the way the sun is shining in on him or if that's an actual tear peering out.

"I still remember when he died." His voice is full of emotion, and as I begin to piece together what he's saying, I finally understand who the ballad was written to honor.

Hee-Man rubs his eye and gives me an apologetic half smile as if to acknowledge his excess of emotions. "My mother fell ill at the news and refused to eat for nearly a week. She was heartbroken. We all were. It felt like the whole thing was a big mistake. None of us believed someone like him would ever pass away."

I did the mental calculations in my head, trying to figure out how old Hee-Man would have been when North Korea's founder Kim Il-Sung died.

"A month after the Great Leader left us, a funeral parade came through our town. Mother was weak and ill, but she forced herself to go. It was raining, but there was more water from our tears than from the sky that day."

I don't make eye contact while I listen to Hee-Man's surprisingly poetic statement.

"That evening, her health took a turn for the worse. A week later, she was gone, following her beloved president to the grave."

I don't know how to respond to this or if I'm even supposed to. The only thing I can even think of comparing

Hee-Man's emotional outpouring to is the way my Grandma Lucy gets in the throes of her religious fervor. So instead of saying anything, I turn my attention once more to the throaty ballad on the radio, and Hee-Man begins to sway again, his shoulder bumping into mine in time with the beat.

CHAPTER 12

We reach Pyongyang as the sun is beginning to set. Most cities I've visited in eastern Asia display what feels like a decade of growth from one year to the next, but Pyongyang looks exactly like it did when I came here as a recent graduate. The same skyscraper stands half-erected, and partially completed construction projects abound with no equipment or crews in sight. The roads are nicer, however, and I figure this must be the closest thing to rush-hour that the city streets see.

At one busy intersection — meaning there are at least two cars waiting at all four stops — a young woman blows her whistle, rolls a baton, and simultaneously directs traffic wearing a miniskirt that might have come straight from a Halloween costume for a sexy policewoman. Hee-Man leans forward to talk to our driver, who pulls the car over next to the curb.

"Please wait here," Hee-Man tells me and jumps out. I have no idea where my guard's courtesy came from or how long

Hee-Man will be doing whatever he set out to do. I glance up to see the driver staring at me nervously in his rearview mirror, and I wonder what he's been told about the redhaired American he's transporting. I steal a furtive glance at the locks on the car door. I could jump out now and get a head start, but of course there's nowhere for me to go and no place for a five-foot-eleven foreigner to hide in a homogenized city like this. The driver is either extra cautious or has some sort of extrasensory perception because he takes his hand slowly off the wheel, and soon I hear the click indicating that I'm locked in here.

Just a few more hours, I think to myself. Whatever formalities I have to go through, whatever forms I have to sign, whatever confessions I have to make, I've already resolved to do it all with rapidity and zeal. Anything to get out of this country. I only wish there was some way I could bring that little homeless boy's picture with me.

Hee-Man is back a moment later, and he taps on the window for the driver to let him in. "Sorry." He smiles as he slips in beside me, holding up a small bag. "I promised my wife I would bring home candy for her and the girls." I wonder if Hee-Man sees this trip to Pyongyang as a paid vacation of sorts. That would certainly explain his more congenial nature and talkative mood.

He situates himself beside me. Even though the backseat

is designed for up to three passengers, he sits in the middle so that we're pressed up together. "Are you hungry?" he asks pleasantly.

For the briefest moment, I allow myself to think that I might be fed more than my few tablespoons of rice and wilted veggies. My mouth waters, but I don't want to get my hopes up too soon.

Hee-Man and the driver exchange a few words, which I can only expect to mean they're debating where we should eat. At the thought of an actual meal, my empty stomach knots itself and rumbles so loudly Hee-Man laughs. Clasping me on my shoulder, he says, "Just a few more minutes, American, and I'm going to treat you to the most delicious seafood you have ever eaten."

I'm unable to determine if my meal truly is as good as Hee-Man promised because I eat it so fast. I'm not actually sure any of it comes into contact with my tongue. Our anonymous driver sits stoically across from us, while Hee-Man hangs out to my left, just as close and snuggly as we'd been in the car. When the waiter brings him his second bottle of soju, I'm convinced my hypothesis is correct, and Hee-Man's business trip to Pyongyang has made him feel like the most fortunate soul in the country. He pours me some alcohol and insists that I take a few shots with him. In my undergrad days, I impressed many a party goer with my ability to hold my liquor, but I must be so weakened from my imprisonment that I feel warmth rushing down my legs and all the way to my toes after my first two shots. I'm compelled to refuse any more soju, which is probably a fairly offensive social blunder, but I insist that Hee-Man is free to continue drinking without me.

He doesn't seem disappointed and orders two more bottles.

Fortunately for me, Hee-Man is as far from what you'd call an angry drunk as anybody you'd care to down shots with, and he's giggling so hard when the two of us pile into the backseat of the car I wonder if his abs will be sore in the morning. He drapes his arm around me as our very sober and still stoic driver lurches the vehicle forward. A small bit of soju from Hee-Man's last bottle splashes onto our laps, and he rubs my leg with his hand as if his palm has turned into an absorbent napkin.

"Sorry, American. I didn't mean to ruin your nice pair of pants."

I assure him that I'm not upset, wondering how concerned I should be that the man who's supposed to lead me to my freedom can't make it through a single sentence without cracking himself up.

"You should have shared more drinks with me, American," he says. His accent is much thicker now that he's drunk. I can hardly understand his words. "Anyway, we'll get you to the hotel and find you a nice change of clothes before your meeting tomorrow."

"Tomorrow?" Any sense of amusement vanishes. "I thought this would happen tonight."

Hee-Man shakes his head. "No, American. That's your problem, my friend. You're far too impatient."

I'd like to see Hee-Man locked up in a room, kept on starvation rations, and interrogated every day, then determine how patient he's feeling a week later.

"But tomorrow?" I hold onto the word as if it were a lifesaver. "We'll get this all sorted out first thing tomorrow?"

Hee-Man shrugs and laughs as the driver takes a turn that spills more soju onto my lap. "Tomorrow or the day after. It's politics, you know."

No, I don't know. "You said all I had to do was come here to Pyongyang, sign some forms, and then go home."

Was he listening? Does he know I've got a sick granny who can't handle stress without having another massive heart attack? Does he know I've got to go see about a girl back home?

Hee-Man finishes off the soju in several noisy gulps and

does me the honor of belching into my face. "Patience, my American friend. These things take time."

I suddenly have the sinking feeling that Hee-Man and I are speaking two entirely different languages. I need to get an exact idea of what to expect over the next few days. "What do you mean by that?" I begin cautiously. "When you say *these things take time*, what things are you referring to?"

Hee-Man tries to suppress another round of giggles. Perhaps he senses I'm no longer in a joking mood. As if I ever were.

"What I am talking about," he begins, his words slurred and his breath about as bad as that stray dog I adopted as a kid, "is your trial. You have been accused of espionage and other crimes against the state. Tomorrow morning I take you to meet your prosecutor."

CHAPTER 13

If I slept at all last night, I certainly don't remember it. As far as I can recall, I spent the entire night in our Pyongyang hotel staring at the ceiling and listening to Hee-Man's drunken snoring. I don't know how long he's going to be stuck to my side like a bad canker sore, but for now we're together. He might be enjoying his vacation in Pyongyang, but I've got to get home.

I run through everything Hee-Man's told me in the past few days. Information about my case, about my supposed crimes. I recall everything he said before we left for Pyongyang. Can I chalk it up to a cross-cultural miscommunication? In his mind, does saying *we're going to Pyongyang so you can fill out some paperwork and go home* actually mean *oh, by the way, you're on trial for espionage*?

None of it makes sense, and I've never been good with uncertainty. I can't sleep, can't relax. My body is exhausted, but my brain's convinced that if I let myself shut my eyes for as long as two seconds, something terrible's going to happen. It's nothing but an evolutionary reflex remnant from the days when man was constantly being hunted by huge, wooly predators, but try telling me that as my body floods me with even more adrenaline.

Hee-Man wakes up, not quite as cheerful as last night when he was giggling like a patient on laughing gas, but if he's got a hangover he's an expert at hiding it. I need to become more like Hee-Man. Keep my emotions so secretive that even I don't know what they are. Enjoy my nice little outing to Pyongyang, ask the driver to stop every so often so I can pick up a souvenir or two, and drink all the soju I want.

Instead, I'm moping because I didn't sleep at all, and I'm brooding because apparently I'm about to stand trial in a state that isn't exactly known as a beacon of human rights. All kinds of rumors I've heard in the past about Pyongyang run through my mind. The leader's uncle and number-two man ripped apart by ravenous dogs. The five top cabinet members purged via anti-aircraft guns fired at close range. The American pastor who visited here a year or two before me — on a tourist visa no less — and was held captive for fourteen months.

Yeah, happy thoughts. When I was at that interrogation center last week, I kept careful track of the passing of time, reminding myself over and over what day it was. Now I don't want to know. It was the end of August when I got arrested. September's coming. I'll miss Grandma Lucy's birthday party. This year was going to be an especially big get-together. And then we're moving quickly on to Thanksgiving, Christmas ... Am I supposed to spend the entire winter here?

And why would Hee-Man have led me to believe we were coming to Pyongyang to secure my release if he really meant I was going to be tried? You don't have to be the director of Amnesty International to realize that an American on trial in Pyongyang, North Korea isn't exactly going to be given the benefit of the doubt. No innocent until proven guilty. For some reason I'm thinking about a case I heard of all the way back when I was in junior high about some college student who got flogged in Singapore for chewing gum in public. Or maybe it was littering. I can't recall the details. All I remember thinking was, *Well, if you knew it was against the law, why'd you do it?*

That's also what people said about that unfortunate college student who was imprisoned in Pyongyang not that long ago. *Why'd he go to a country as backwards as North Korea if he wasn't asking for trouble?* Some even assumed he really must have been a spy like the North Korean government claimed.

I wonder now what they're saying about me.

He should have never crossed the border. He got what's coming to him.

Of course, that's only if they believe the official North Korean report that I sneaked in here voluntarily. Which is probably what they're circulating now to all the media.

If they've even said anything about me at all. It's just as likely that nobody knows I'm here. And then what? Do I just remain a prisoner and die anonymously? What about Grandma Lucy? That woman's already survived a major heart attack. I can't stand the thought that my arrest is going to put her through another one. I really can't.

And I shouldn't have to. So excuse me if I'm not Mr. Chipper when Hee-Man smiles and asks me what I'd like for breakfast. What I'd like is for him to wipe that smug smirk off his face and deal with me honestly for once.

Is that so much to ask?

I was forthright with him. Is it too outrageous for me to expect him to possibly return the favor? I told him everything, all about that little homeless boy in my photograph. And he seemed like he believed me. So what happened?

"You're not feeling good?" he asks ever so helpfully. "Too much to drink last night?"

I shake my head. I wish my troubles were as simple and mundane as a hangover. I'd take a hangover every stinking day of my life if it meant I could hop on a plane and fly back home.

The worst part is thinking about all the people worrying about me. Like my girlfriend/not-girlfriend. The fact that we broke up has everything to do with her religious convictions and nothing to do with how either of us feel about each other. Because if we were just going by how we felt, we'd have ended the summer engaged. You know, if it weren't for my getting arrested and all that.

#Plottwist, right?

Of course, there's everyone else in my family, too. Not just Grandma Lucy. There's my sister Alayna. She's got to be beside herself with anxiety. All my aunts, uncles, cousins. Grandma Lucy's the matriarch of a clan of hundreds. No, I'm not exaggerating. And when they hear what's happened to me …

I don't know how Grandma Lucy's going to survive this. I don't mean to sound arrogant either. But she's a frail, fragile woman. What does it do to a little old lady to learn that her grandson's being held in a North Korean jail? Whatever it is can't be good.

I've got to get out of here. Got to get myself back home.

"You are ready for breakfast?" Hee-Man asks, and I snap at him.

"I'm not ready for anything except to leave this disgusting place." I wait, fully expecting him to spit in my face or slap me across the cheek or put my hands behind my back and order me to stand in a corner for dissing his homeland, but he thinks I'm talking about the hotel.

"Yes, I think I will request different accommodations for the rest of our time here."

My ears perk up. This is the first I've heard of Hee-Man's actually staying with me. "What do you mean? You're sticking around?"

He nods and beams proudly. "Yes, American. I requested the assignment myself."

What am I supposed to say to that? How flattered I am? It clearly seems to be what he's waiting for, but I'm not going to oblige him. "I thought you said this would be short," I grumble. "Just some formalities."

"It will be short," he explains. "Just a few weeks to go over your statements with the prosecutor, and then directly to the trial."

Is he trying to make me feel better? He's seriously got to be the least motivating motivational speaker I've ever heard.

"That's fast in your book?" I ask.

He glances around the room. "What book?"

"Never mind. So you'll be around until it starts? Until the trial, I mean?"

He straightens his spine. "If I do my job well, they may even let me stay on for the trial itself."

If I had a dog treat, I'd be tempted to toss it his way. That's how proudly he's beaming at me, like he wants me to scratch him behind his ears and croon, *now who's a good little North Korean officer?*

I'm so sick of all these changes in plans, all these false hopes. False starts.

"You do not look happy," he observes with his usual degree of usefulness.

"I'm not." It's no use getting upset with him. In my logical mind, I know this. Hee-Man's doing his job, enjoying his little business trip before he gets to go home and give his wife and daughters all the pretty gifts he buys for them on the government's dime. But I'm the one now awaiting trial for crimes I didn't commit. It would be infinitely easier if he hadn't led me to believe I was about to go home in the first place. There's nothing worse than disappointment.

Shattered hopes.

I can't take it.

"Can we go out?" I ask.

"Out?" He says the word as if he's all of a sudden forgotten the most basic of English.

"Out. For a walk. Somewhere. I need the fresh air."

He nods. "A walk. Very good. I will tell our minders where we are going."

So we have a pair of minders now. Why doesn't that surprise me? Will they let Hee-Man and me venture out alone, or will they follow along and make up an entire entourage?

Right now, I don't care. I need to get out of this hotel room. I need to move my legs, to think.

I need to figure out how I'm going to survive this trial.

CHAPTER 14

"So tell me what you know about this prosecutor," I ask Hee-Man once we're outside.

Apparently, my guard must think I want to know what the lawyer's called. "His name is Mr. Kim."

If I were having a good day, I'd crack a joke. *Another Kim? Is he your brother? Any relationship to old Jong-Il?* But I'm not having a good day, not by anyone's definition of the term.

I've just spent seven days stuck in some backwards holding cell in North Korea being interrogated because I happened to find myself drugged and shanghaied over the border. Now I'm in Pyongyang, where I'll waste weeks as a prisoner getting ready for my trial, and assuming I'm found guilty (because this is North Korea, where human rights don't even exist), I'll be faced with hard labor or torture or execution. Honestly, of the three I don't even know which would be worse. Not that I'll have a say in the matter, I'm sure. I've opposed the death penalty my entire life, but compared to the alternatives ...

I tell my brain I'm getting ahead of myself, but you can't blame me for thinking like this. What would you choose? The worst part is in the back of my head I hear Grandma Lucy's Bible verses like she's standing in front of me reciting them.

Do not worry about tomorrow. Each day can worry about itself.

I doubt I'm getting the translation exactly right, but I know I've got the gist.

Great advice, Grandma Lucy. Now you want to explain to me how in the world I'm supposed to keep from worrying?

In the back of my head, I'm recalling a conversation I had with her at some point last year. She told me she'd been praying for my salvation. Now that in itself is certainly not newsworthy, as I'm convinced that Grandma Lucy prays multiple times an hour for my wayward soul. But she told me something else that day. "If you keep rejecting God after all the ways he's blessed you, he might start to withhold some of those blessings if that's what it takes to get your attention."

I didn't ask her what she meant. I'd gleaned enough from all those church services she dragged me to when I was younger that I understood just what she was saying. If I won't ask Jesus into my heart because my life is so good I feel like I don't need him, well, what's going to stop God from making my life miserable until I turn to him?

And she wonders why early on in my college days I came to the conclusion that the God of the Bible, at least as he's described by his Bible-believing children in America, is a cosmic abuser.

But now her words come rushing through my memory banks. Taunting me. Grandma Lucy's off her Holy Spirit rocker, but if there is a God, would he seriously condemn me to prison in North Korea just to force me to repent? How is that different from the sociopath who bashes his girlfriend's head into the wall just to make sure she remembers that he's the only one who would ever love her, ever treat her as good as he does? And yet she stays with him, longs for his protection, just like there's a primitive, juvenile instinct inside me that wants to lose myself in the throes of prayer like Grandma Lucy does. Not that I'd even know how to get back into it after all these years, but I'm sure I could try. I was fairly religious growing up, professing all the Bible truths Grandma Lucy wanted me to profess. I wasn't going behind her back, saying words I knew were lies. I think if I were to truly assess my psychological and spiritual state in those days, I was a believer just like she was. Well, not just like she was, because let's face it, the world isn't big enough for more than one Grandma Lucy, but you know what I mean.

It was as early as my first week at Harvard when I stepped back and realized every single thing I believed about God was what Grandma Lucy told me to believe. I had every reason as a child to expect that she was speaking the truth, so I accepted what she said at face value. I think Grandma Lucy regrets ever sending me off to college in the first place no matter how many times I tried to explain that I'm so much better off for having the education I received.

I felt terribly guilty attending a school like Harvard. Me, the white boy from middle-class America, who never knew poverty, who grew up with neighbors who were just as white and middle class as I was. My upbringing was more rural than my counterparts from suburbia (I was the only one in my first-year dorm who knew how to milk a goat), but how many students of color could have benefited from what I received? How many students from the inner city enrolled in the same courses and sat in the same lecture halls I did?

By the end of my first year, I was so heavy with shame I almost didn't go back. It was actually Grandma Lucy who convinced me otherwise, which is somewhat ironic, but she had more to teach me about privilege, class, and white guilt than any of my professors could.

When I explained that I was planning to give up my spot at Harvard so that an underprivileged student could take my place, she pulled out that worn New Testament of hers and turned to one of the gospels and showed me those words in red, the ones where Jesus says, "To him who has been given much, much will be demanded." I'd seen Spiderman by that point, and it's exactly what Uncle Ben says: *With great power comes great responsibility.*

"You don't need to be ashamed of being white," she said, and I fully expected her to go off spouting all the great things my western-European ancestors did in the past. You know, bringing Christianity and measles over to the New World to destroy native culture and decimate the population, defending civilization from Islamic aggression (because we've all seen how much of a safer world this is post 9-11), and so on. But she didn't.

"As a white man, doors will open for you that others would have to fight tirelessly to walk through. People will listen to you and accept you as an authority. And you can use your platform to effect great change."

So maybe my little old granny isn't quite as backwards and anti-progressive as some might think.

She kept up her lecture for quite a while, even though I caught on to the premise right away. What if I stopped feeling guilty for my inherent privilege and instead used my advantage to speak up for those who were unable to speak for themselves? She also helpfully pointed out that Harvard rarely accepts transfer students, so as lofty as my plan might be to step down so another less fortunate student might take my place, it wouldn't help anyone. It would be like seeing a man with only one leg and chopping my own off instead of using the two legs I've got to make his lot — and mine — better.

These are the memories I've got running through my head as Hee-Man and I walk the Pyongyang sidewalks, followed a good ten paces behind by our minders. If I had a really good sense of imagination, I could picture myself as the President, Hee-Man as my Vice, and all our followers as the Secret Service officers here to protect us. Except I know these minders aren't here for my personal safety. They're trying to make sure I don't make a run for it. As if I had anywhere I could hide in a city like this. I've resolved to ignore them, but so far I'm not doing that great of a job.

At least I can enjoy the fresh air. Hee-Man apparently doesn't understand the point of walking for the sake of walking and keeps stopping in front of each and every store we pass and asking if I want to go in. I try to explain I'm not here for souvenirs or food or anything else. I just want to clear my head. Well, even if he doesn't get it, I'm glad to be outside. I've spent far too many days already cramped in that little interrogation room, and by the sound of it there's not much more in store for me besides more questions, more small rooms, more cramped quarters.

Lucky me.

Maybe it really was Grandma Lucy who prayed me into this situation. I might not believe in the exact same God she does, but that doesn't mean I've discounted the power of prayer. Like that time in high school when my tooth was so rotted they thought they were going to have to pull the whole thing, but when they got me all prepped, it turned out it was nothing more than your everyday run of the mill cavity. Drill, fill, and my tooth and I were both good to go.

When I got home, Grandma Lucy said she'd been praying that I wouldn't need the extraction. She wasn't even surprised when I told her what happened.

"That's what you can expect when you pray," was all she had to say.

So if Grandma Lucy's convinced that I won't turn to God unless he makes my life a living nightmare, what's to stop her from praying for me to be completely miserable? It's backward logic, but it makes perfect sense. If you're the type of crazy old lady who believes that every person who dies without asking Jesus to forgive their sins is destined to go to a fiery hell, and you're similarly convinced that if your grandson's life gets horrible enough that he'll have no choice but to convert to Christianity, then watching him suffer for a little bit on earth is vastly preferable than seeing his soul condemned for all eternity. Get what I'm saying?

So even if I don't believe in her God, I believe in the power of her prayers, at least on some level, and I'm livid that she might have wished this terror on me, her grandson. What woman does that? You've got to be a certain kind of sick and twisted.

Up until this week, I've rolled my eyes at Grandma Lucy's prayers. Now they're about all I can think of. The one comfort I cling to isn't that the US government's going to dump all its resources into getting me home. I already gave you my impression on the current administration. What I'm holding onto, the hope that's keeping me sane during these miserable, sleepless nights, is that if Grandma Lucy's prayers were powerful enough to get me into this mess, they may also be effective in getting me out.

Because if they don't, I'm going to be stuck in this country until I die.

And that's not an option I'm willing to explore. Not even in my dreams.

So pray on, Grandma Lucy. I'm pretty sure my entire life, and maybe even my soul's eternal destiny, is depending on it.

CHAPTER 15

I try to avoid extremes in the drama department when I can help it. My photography advisor in grad school described my style as *subtly understated but not to the point where the message gets completely lost.* Whatever that means. Bottom line is I don't overdo it, not in my writing, not in my photography, and (at least until this week) not in my personal life.

Try telling that to me now, as I'm in yet another hotel room shaking the hand of yet another Mr. Kim, this one my prosecuting attorney.

It's a little after lunchtime, and I'm only now sitting down to meet my prosecutor. Hee-Man is the epitome of deference and professionalism when he introduces me to the man charged with accusing me before a Pyongyang court. For the first time in my life, I'm kicking myself for not pursuing my original major of international relations. I imagine any crash course in diplomacy could be helpful in a setting like this. I still don't quite know what Hee-Man's doing here. He's like my court-appointed liaison, my defense attorney, and my personal bodyguard all wrapped up into one. He's soaking up this extra attention like a self-inflating air mattress, and I'm not going to complain. Quite frankly, I could use a friend in my court.

Mr. Kim's all business. No chitchat, no deeply probing personal questions like *how are you?* Just the basics. He's got a stack of paper in front of him, and I recognize my handwriting on the college-ruled pages.

"So, you are a journalist."

I nod. His English is even better than Hee-Man's, and I have to strain to detect any accent whatsoever.

"You graduated from Harvard University."

I nod again and glance at Hee-Man. Is this what I'm supposed to be doing? He gives me a smile that's surprisingly reassuring.

Mr. Kim studies my writing before looking at me over the top of my pages. "Who is Nick Fury?"

I shake my head. In a few years, I might look back at what I did and crack myself up to the point where I split a rib or something, but right now, I wish I'd never written that stupid Avengers joke. "It's nothing," I say. "I wasn't being serious."

I reach for the paper, but Mr. Kim snatches it out of my

grasp as if I were a kidnapper about to steal his baby right from out of his arms. "I didn't mean that story," I try to explain. "It's all made up."

Hee-Man jumps to my defense, saying something in Korean. If I had to wager a translation, it'd be something like *Please forgive the stupid American. You'll have to overlook this writing. He was acting particularly naughty on this day and was made to stand in the corner for several hours. I oversaw his punishment myself, so I should know what I'm talking about.*

Mr. Kim sets those pages aside into a special folder that I hope I won't see in the future. Somewhere in the back of my head I hear my sixth-grade schoolteacher scolding, *Ian, all your jokes and pranks and antics are going to catch up with you one day, young man.*

Maybe if I get out of here, I'll look her up and tell her she was right.

"So you came to North Korea in the past?" Mr. Kim wants me to tell him everything about my previous trip to Pyongyang and even asks me if I remember the names of my two minders.

I don't.

"And the little boy you took a picture of? Do you maintain regular contact with him?"

"What? No. He was just a little kid. We never even spoke."

Mr. Kim frowns and has a hushed conversation with Hee-Man. I don't know why they bother to whisper, first of all because I can still hear every word they're saying but even more importantly because they're carrying on in Korean.

In the end, Mr. Kim makes me restate several times that I'd never met this little boy or had any contact with him before or after I took his picture. When I'm made to repeat it in the tenth different way, I finally lose my temper and turn to Hee-Man. "I've told him I don't know the kid. What's this all about?"

More Korean. I feel like I did years ago when my then-girlfriend always wanted me to watch foreign flicks with her. I'd like to find a remote that will give Mr. Kim and Hee-Man subtitles or something so I can follow what they're saying.

Hee-Man's frowning. He leans over and whispers to me, "You swear you do not know this boy?"

"Yes, I swear. Why? What's the big deal?"

Hee-Man shakes his head. "Apparently he was found with the canister of film we developed. We assumed that you were using him to spread your propaganda."

Is everyone in this blasted country paranoid? Do they all need to start popping anti-psychotics or something?

"No, he was just a kid. I saw him digging in the dirt and decided to take his picture. I'm sorry," I tell them even though I'm not. I may never see that photograph again once I'm sentenced, but I don't care.

I took it. And it exists in my mind. They can erase the original, shred up the negative, delete any digital copies they might have made, but they'll never take away the expression from that boy's haunted eyes. So I stretch the truth when I apologize one more time and tell them how remorseful I am for breaking their rules so many years ago by taking one photograph.

Hee-Man doesn't look happy with me, and I've decided to gauge my situation based on his expression since Mr. Kim's looked like he's wanted to strangle me since the moment we met. I know I won't get answers from him, so I turn to Hee-Man, the closest thing I have to a friend in this whole country.

Another one of those plot twists, I guess.

"What is it?" I ask. "Tell me." I know there's something going on but can't imagine what it is.

"That boy was arrested. We … our people assumed he was working for you." He's almost mumbling the words. There's no sign of the happy little drunk who snored away in the hotel bed next to me last night.

"You arrested a helpless homeless kid?" I stop myself. Apparently I'm not supposed to have realized this boy was homeless because according to the Party line, there have never been any impoverished children anywhere in North Korea.

Of course.

I'm ignoring Mr. Kim and focusing all my attention now on Hee-Man. "You arrested him?" I repeat, my tone dripping in anger and accusation.

Great. I ruined that boy's life. After all the attention I've always paid to cultural sensitivity, all the classes I've taken on ethics in journalism, and I've done the unpardonable. I've destroyed an innocent bystander for the sake of a photograph.

What kind of award or recognition is worth knowing a little kid was sent to rot in jail because of me?

"Where is he now?" I demand. "What'd you do with him?"

"We have programs ..." Hee-Man begins, but I'm in no mood for his politically correct half-truths.

"Where is he?" I shout. It's been years since I ruined this boy's life, but I have to know what became of him.

Hee-Man shakes his head. "I really do not know. I am sorry."

Sorry? For what? For telling me that I sentenced a poor little kid to jail? For a moment, I wonder if maybe at least in prison he would have been protected from the elements and better fed than he was on the streets, but I know from firsthand experience exactly how much food North Koreans dish out to their prisoners. The poor kid would have been better off digging for roots.

Better off if he'd never met me.

It's going to take me a lifetime to get over this. A lifetime of penance and regret. How could I have been so selfish? I never even thought about what might have happened to that boy. And what was he doing with my film anyway? Unless he saw me drop it and was curious …

How could I have been so stupid? Suddenly I feel like whatever punishment I'm about to receive is deserved. What else should you expect when you waltz into a country that's not your own and with a single photograph you steal a boy's entire childhood?

They better not have put him in a labor camp. I'd like to think I was blissfully ignorant enough to believe there were no kids in those atrocious conditions, but I've interviewed enough defectors to know that's not the case. Is that poor creature even alive now? And how am I supposed to live with the guilt of his incarceration on my conscience?

It's so typically American of me, I'd laugh if I weren't so sure I was about to puke. Storm into some village, see a kid in poverty, take a photograph to send home, get my Pulitzer and my name recognition and my Twitter followers, never once thinking how I ruined a child's future by my one act of selfishness and stupidity.

I'm ashamed of everything about me right now. Ashamed of that brazen, ethnocentric Americanness that I can't seem to shake no matter how hard I try. Ashamed of my privilege that made it impossible for me to even wonder if my actions might hurt a boy that young and helpless. I'm so disgusted with myself I'm ready to face my trial now, but Mr. Kim just picks up the next page of my so-called confessions, ready to go through every word, line by line.

This is my penance, I suppose, for now at least. And it's probably going to get far worse from here on out.

And at this moment, I'm convinced I deserve everything coming my way.

CHAPTER 16

"I think that went well." Hee-Man is heartily eating a bowl of noodle soup as we sit together in our hotel room. The sun set hours ago, but we've just now finished the first round of meetings with the prosecutor.

"That went well?" I repeat incredulously. In spite of how famished I was after my week of prison food, I have no appetite at all.

Hee-Man must perceive I'm still thinking about that little boy. "Don't worry too much," he says. "Many boys escape the work factories. It happens all the time."

This is the first I've heard of work factories and the closest admission I've heard from anyone in North Korea that their citizens might not be living in the perfect little utopic bubble they want us all to believe exists, but I'm not going to press the issue. I've already done enough damage.

"At least in the factories he would have been given shelter and food." Hee-Man's reciting the excuses I've already tried unsuccessfully to buy into. If life was so good in these factories, there wouldn't be homeless kids in North Korea to begin with. They'd all be clamoring to go there. I feel about as progressive as Ebenezer Scrooge himself: *Are there no prisons? Are there no workhouses?*

And I loathe myself.

If Grandma Lucy were here, she'd tell me this is all false guilt. And trust me, true to her conservative Christian morals, that woman knows how to dish up plenty of the real stuff. Believing in evolution? That's a sin. Refusing to condemn homosexuals as perverse individuals with no moral compass? Nearly as bad as the act of homosexuality itself. And since in her Bible, having sexual desires is the same thing as sleeping around with every single person you find attractive, I can guarantee you there isn't anyone worthy of the salvation she talks about so passionately.

It's interesting to think how Christians rail on and on about certain kinds of sin while completely ignoring others. That same pastor who's telling his congregation to go out and share the gospel with all their neighbors and friends is wearing shoes, socks, pants, and a collared shirt that were all made by slaves, the vast majority of them underage, in conditions that would force an OCEA manager to come down with a migraine. But as long as all his congregants go out and drag a few more converts-in-waiting through the church doors, it's all good. The same youth leader who spends his Wednesday nights berating teen girls for wearing too much makeup or rolling their skirts too short or showing the tiniest hint of their figure has an incurable porn addiction, but he's still allowed to make a fourteen-year-old girl feel dirty because she doesn't wear a full-length jumpsuit when she goes to the beach with her family.

I could go on and on. I really could, except I know it won't get us anywhere. It won't free that boy I condemned to a life of slavery, and it won't help me get out of Pyongyang any more quickly. I just get so frustrated with Christians because if they took a good, long look at what that precious Bible of theirs actually says, they'd become the most progressive movement the world has ever seen. Instead, they make fun of social justice, act like it's some kind of new fad or trend and not something their own God talks about hundreds of times in their holy book, and they insist on remaining so inwardly focused that they don't even see the poverty and injustice that's permeating their own neighborhoods.

They rail against sex before marriage, but they have no idea how many girls are forced into prostitution in their own back yards, and if the sordid details are discovered, the victim is written off as some sex-crazed fiend who's only in the life because "she must like it." Meanwhile, they ignore the statistics that stand condemning them. Exhibit A: Being a foster kid increases your chances of being prostituted tenfold. Exhibit B? If every church — not even every individual family in every church, just every church — decided to care for one foster kid, there would be no US foster system as we know it. No more kids waiting for families.

But these Christians, like the ones at my Grandma's church, are too busy policing who's sleeping with who to make any stinking difference whatsoever. It sickens me. All of it. Except right now I have no one to talk to about these things. Hee-Man's still offering sweet little platitudes about the boy in my photograph, assuring me that even though the factories are compulsory for kids who fall into trouble with the police, the work really isn't so bad for them, not if you compare it to life on the streets.

He doesn't know. How could he? He's just as brainwashed by propaganda as the rest of them, and yet I get the feeling that if he really understood what was going on in the world he'd be different. An activist. I don't know what makes me think this way. A hint of compassion about him, I suppose. Like when he thrusts our one bowl of noodle soup into my hands and insists that I finish it off. He's even left two pieces of some kind of mystery meat in there for me.

I'm so stressed out and I loathe myself and my situation so much right now that eating's the last thing on my mind, but I recognize that he's looking out for me in the only way he knows how. He's like my Aunt Connie. You come home from school crying because your best friend got beaten up because he's scrawny and wears glasses? She thrusts a plate of cookies, a ginormous cinnamon roll, and a tall cup of goat milk in front of you and tells you that you'll feel better once you eat up.

So I take Hee-Man's leftover soup and force myself to swallow down as much as I can. It's pretty good. Far better than rice and moldy veggies, but I can't stop wondering what that little boy in my photograph has to eat tonight.

If he's even alive.

It's like the summer I came home from my first year of college crippled with guilt for being white. Detesting the fact that the very land I grew up on had been stolen from Native Americans, that while my ancestors came to the New World, got rich, and flourished, whole tribes in Africa were stolen and made to suffer unthinkable torments on plantations owned by horrible men who looked like me. While I grew up with every educational and vocational opportunity laid out wide open before me, descendants of slaves were forced to fight for every single inch of progress they received at the risk of getting lynched or waking up to find a cross burning in their front yard.

"There's nothing you can do to change your genetics," Grandma Lucy told me when I falteringly tried to explain how I felt. "All you can do is take the blessings God's given you and use them to further his kingdom."

By which she probably meant I should become a pastor or missionary, but I took it to mean something else. As part of my quest to atone for the sins of my ancestors, I could use my privilege to stand up for those who didn't yet have a voice for themselves. Which is why I went into journalism.

It sounded so noble at the time. Until I learned that the best photograph I'd ever taken or ever will take led to the imprisonment of an innocent boy.

If Mr. Kim knocked on the door right now and told me there was a firing squad ready to save the state some time and put me out of my misery, I'd march ahead and never look back. I once overheard my Aunt Connie telling a friend that she thought her definition of being a mom was always feeling guilty you weren't doing enough. I suppose that's how I feel about being a socially-conscious white male. Guilty that I'm not doing enough, that I'm wasting my life, fattening myself on my blessings of privilege while others suffer around me.

Hee-Man clasps my shoulder. "Be happy," he tells me. "The pre-trial period should only last a few weeks." And now I finally understand his excitement. He's going to stay here at least until the trial starts, and he's planning to milk his government gravy-train job for all its worth. I'm surprised he hasn't broken out the soju again.

I hand him my empty bowl. I've saved one last piece of meat because the first was so chewy and I couldn't entirely pinpoint the taste. I wasn't about to add eating something like dog or cat to my already riddled conscience.

"I'm going to bed," I tell him. "You can have the last bite."

I crawl under the blankets, not even bothering to change because in all their wisdom and generosity, my captors haven't thought to give me any extra pairs of clothes or pajamas yet.

"Good night," I mumble. As I shut my eyes, I watch Hee-Man glance at me, pick up the chopsticks, and toss meat into his mouth.

His loud chewing is the last sound I hear before drifting off to sleep.

CHAPTER 17

The next several days all blur into one another as I meet with Mr. Kim, who wants to go over every single sentence I wrote during my initial interrogations. The only thing he doesn't seem to dwell on is my statement that I was drugged and smuggled over the border. I know the official line is that I'm some sort of crazed journalist with a death wish who decided to take my life into my hands and sneak into North Korea. I hope people back home aren't really buying that bologna.

Hee-Man, also known as my new soulmate (at least as far as he's concerned), hangs out with us during the majority of our interviews, barely speaking unless it's to encourage me to elaborate a little bit more. The rare times he goes out to do a little shopping or sight-seeing, I have to admit I miss him. I wonder if Grandma Lucy's been praying that God would send me a friend.

I've signed at least two dozen different variations of the same confession by now. I'm sure most Americans live by the adage that you don't sign any legally-binding agreement without going through the fine print or consulting an attorney, but that's not the way things work around here. In Pyongyang, if you don't sign, you don't eat.

I'm still being treated all right. Hee-Man no longer appears to be a fan of toddler-level discipline, and I haven't been made to stand in the corner at all since we arrived in Pyongyang. I suppose that for all my alleged crimes, the people who know me must not consider me a huge threat because I'm not handcuffed either, and at night it's just me and Hee-Man in our little hotel room. I suppose they all know that even if I were to escape, there'd be no place for me to hide.

I suppose it's a good thing I've been studying this part of the world since college. My documentary on North Korean refugees in China is almost entirely edited. I know that it's possible they've ransacked my place on the other side of the border and confiscated my work, but everything's backed up in multiple clouds. Worst case scenario is they get into my computer and my backup accounts and delete everything, but I still have the raw interviews at home. It just means another nine months of edits, but what's nine months when you're living in freedom, right?

I try not to think about the passing of time. I don't ask what day it is and try not to keep track of dates. Grandma

Lucy's probably already had her big birthday party, and I'm sure there were lots of prayers for me. I'm definitely not the only one of Grandma Lucy's hundred-plus descendants who isn't a Christian, but I often feel like I'm the one she prays for most. Maybe because she helped raise me for basically all of my working memory. It's almost a game between me and my other cousins. Who does Grandma pray for most?

I think my sister Alayna gets bragging rights, though, because Grandma Lucy alphabetizes her prayer list so she can keep it all straight in her mind, and Alayna always comes first. It would take a savant to rattle off the names of all our cousins, but I know there's got to be a dozen or more whose names come before Ian in alphabetical order.

But I'm still happy to know Grandma Lucy's praying for me.

At night when my interviews with Mr. Kim are over, Hee-Man and I sit around chatting about as many random topics as he can come up with. I'm surprised the minders let us spend so much time together. Aren't they worried I'll corrupt him with my Western propaganda? All I can guess is he goes back and reports everything to his superiors. They probably have our room bugged too, so this friendship we've developed is all part of their ploy to get me to break. To incriminate myself and prove I'm a spy sent here straight from the CIA.

It makes me sad, not that they don't trust me but that they're using Hee-Man this way.

Or maybe he's using me. I suppose it just depends on how you look at it.

Either way, I feel sorry for the man.

"You know what I have decided about you, American?" he says one night. He'd been so quiet I thought he was already asleep.

"What have you decided?" My feet are sticking out from underneath my blankets. That's how small this bed is, but it's still more comfortable than sleeping on a cold floor in my boxers.

"I've decided that you are not a bad person."

What are you supposed to say to that? *Gee thanks. You're pretty swell yourself.*

Hee-Man rolls over and from the moonlight slipping in from the window, I can see the tiredness in his eyes. "You were just brainwashed." He lets out a yawn "It is not your fault. If you'd had the chance to grow up here and to know the truth, you would be a totally different person."

I sigh. "You know what? I think you're probably right about that last part," I answer, but my friend doesn't respond.

He's already fallen asleep.

CHAPTER 18

As hard as I'm trying to forget about the passing of time, my body and brain are still locked into a seven-day cycle. It's a hard habit to break even in conditions like this. I think I've been in Pyongyang a little less than a week. I refuse to add up how long I've been imprisoned from the beginning. Part of me still thinks that if I just ignore the calendar, they'll let me go and I'll find out I didn't miss Grandma Lucy's big birthday bash after all.

Funny the things you focus on when every single freedom of yours has been stripped away.

I would have thought I'd be more worried about the documentary I just spent hundreds of hours editing in China. But nope. Here I am, stuck in a Pyongyang hotel room, which may as well be a jail cell for all the movement I'm allowed, and my biggest concern is missing my grandma's party.

I wonder if it's a good thing that I can still manage to surprise myself.

Mr. Kim and I are finished for the day. It's just me and Hee-Man now. I don't know if it's because he's running short on cash or what, but it's been a few days since my friend's gone out for drinks or brought any soju back to our room. That doesn't stop him from being as talkative as ever though.

"Tell me something about America," he says. "What do the little kids like to do? The four- and five-year-olds? What is life like for them?"

I explain the intricacies of little league, walk him through the finer points of show and tell, and next thing I know we're talking about Pixar films.

"Have you seen the one with the fish?" he asks.

I'm surprised that anyone knows about Nemo here. My understanding was all foreign media was off limits.

I nod, and he sighs nostalgically. "That was a good one."

"So you've seen it?" This goes against my suspicion that our room is tapped. If foreign movies are illegal here, even ones as innocuous as *Finding Nemo*, why would he admit to watching it on a recording?

Hee-Man gives me an enthusiastic nod. "It was very well made. I like the part when his dad finds him again."

"Yeah. That's kind of the point."

"I would like to show my daughters *Nemo*," he admits,

and somehow I feel like I should change the subject. I don't want my friend to incriminate himself in a burst of sentimentality.

"You are a moviemaker in America?" Hee-Man asks.

"Not that kind of movie." I explain the difference between journalism and Hollywood, but somehow I still get the feeling Hee-Man pictures me in some mansion with my director cap on shouting *cut* as we record a scene, me and my staff of hundreds.

The furniture's so light here Hee-Man can actually scoot his bed next to mine as easily as if it were a folding chair. We're still in our respective spaces, except now his face is about six inches away from mine. "If I found us an American movie to watch, would you like that?"

I glance around the room. Is this a trap? Is this some sort of bizarre loyalty test?

"Wouldn't that get you in trouble?"

Hee-Man grins. "No, I know the minders on watch tonight. They would not report us," he says, thus confirming two of my suspicions: we are being watched, and Hee-Man does consider me his friend.

I prop myself up on my elbow. "What movie do you have in mind?" I hope it's not *Nemo*. Nothing against kid film, but if we're going to be watching Pixar, I'd rather stick with a true classic like *Toy Story*. Whoever thought to put Tom Hanks in the roll of Woody is an eternal genius.

Hee-Man pulls a flash drive out of his back pocket and squints. "I don't know how to say it." He holds it out to me, and I read the handwriting in about size 4 font that's etched on the side.

"*Armageddon?*"

"You know it?" he asks happily.

Classic disaster film from the '90s? Of course I know it. "It's a good one." The words leave my mouth and send Hee-Man into a massive grin. "How'd you get this?"

He holds his fingers up to his lips, and I hope he knows what he's doing. I suppose my neck's already on the line as it is, but I don't want Hee-Man to get in trouble on my account. My reasons are as selfish as they are altruistic. I don't want to share my time and my room and my existence with anyone but him.

Hee-Man pulls a laptop out from under his mattress, and I wonder how many hours he invested into this little stunt. It's like we're ten-year-olds sneaking a peek at our first horror film at a slumber party, terrified that any moment our parents are going to wake up and get us into really big trouble.

"So this movie, how do you say it again?"

"*Armageddon*," I answer and give a brief rundown of what I remember of the term from my Bible-believing days. "But don't worry," I tell him, "this movie has nothing to do with religion. It's about outer space and astronauts."

Hee-Man's smiling like I did as a kid when I was eventually told I could keep the stray dog who wandered into our yard. He sets the laptop on the foot of my bed and before I know it he's sitting next to me. All we need is a bag of popcorn to share and this would turn into a real sleepover.

"You do not mind if I put on captions, do you?" he asks. "It is easier for me to follow the English that way." I'm surprised at this implied confession that this isn't Hee-Man's first foreign film, and I'm just as surprised at how quickly he manages to get the captions onto the screen.

And then before I know it, I'm watching Bruce Willis putting golf balls onto a Green Peace protest boat, and if it weren't for the kink in my neck and the fact that I'm snuggling up with a middle-aged Korean man whose sole job is to keep me from running away, I might even be able to convince myself I'm happy.

CHAPTER 19

I've never been in the habit of watching movies with the captions on before. At first, I'm annoyed, but I find that even though I've seen this film five or six times at least, I'm catching things now I never noticed before.

Like did you know that Harry actually raised AJ? It adds a layer and a depth to Harry and AJ's relationship I wouldn't have caught if my film buddy didn't prefer to read the words in English.

It's taking us about twice as long as it should to get through the movie because Hee-Man's pausing at the rate of about once every three minutes to ask me questions. Why would the government waste a nuclear weapon on an asteroid? Wouldn't they want to keep it for their own protection? Why would a Russian astronaut risk his life to help people who weren't his kinsmen? Won't he get in trouble with the higher-ups back home? How can Americans trust their government at all when this movie itself proves that Washington DC is in the habit of shamelessly lying to its citizens?

"Hee-Man, it's a movie." Eventually I steal the remote from him so he can't keep pausing it incessantly. "You're not really supposed to believe any of it."

He shakes his head. "That's why your country is so good at controlling you."

As reluctant as I am, I'm forced to watch *Armageddon* now through the eyes of a North Korean guard who's been taught his entire life that the American government is in the business of brainwashing its people. As far as Hee-Man sees it, this film is just a high-budget propaganda piece about patriotism.

Or something like that.

Once I seize control of the remote, it's a little easier. I still have to explain certain Americanisms to my pal, who has no idea what a loan shark is and who now believes that every single American city has seedy strip clubs lined up on every corner.

"See that man? He is not a good father. His kid doesn't know him." Hee-Man points to the screen at one of the minor characters.

"Just watch the movie," I mumble.

I hate to admit it to myself, but parts of the story are tearing me up inside. And not the ones you'd expect either. You want to know what starts me off? When Bear, this huge beast of a man, jumps onto the table, strips down to his tiger-striped underwear, and starts dancing for all the NASA doctors who are inspecting him.

Hee-Man's glancing at me, I'm sure appalled at the indecency of it all, but I'm getting choked up. That man looks so happy.

And so indescribably free.

And the whole Harry-AJ drama is getting to me far more than ever before. I can only guess it's because I'm processing something about my own relationship with my father, but why would I be thinking about him now? He died years ago, I was sad, I got over it. But I can hardly stand to watch the scenes where Harry and AJ fight, especially now that I've realized just how much like Harry's son AJ really was.

I manage to keep control over my emotions well enough that I don't think Hee-Man suspects what's going on, and by the time the crew lands on the asteroid, my friend is so invested in the storyline he forgets to ask me any more questions. Finally I'm able to enjoy the movie on my own terms and in my own way. No more questions, no more pauses. I've gotten used to the captions too, so they're not so distracting as they were at first.

It's the most dramatic part of the movie, where Harry and his team have to drill a nuke down deep enough into an asteroid so that they can destroy it before it collides with earth. There's explosions, tension, and if you were to judge by Hee-Man's reaction, it's suspenseful enough to literally take your breath away.

But here I am thinking about that little homeless kid.

I still haven't gotten over it. I doubt I ever will. One of the only things that's made this past week or so in Pyongyang bearable is the knowledge that I deserve everything coming my way. If I don't get out of here, if I end up getting sentenced at my trial and can never leave the country again, I wonder if that will somehow atone for what I did to ruin that boy's life.

You could always hope, right?

We're toward the end of the movie now. Hee-Man is practically sitting on my lap, and he's gripping my arm when it comes time for the team to draw straws to see which one of the characters will have to stay behind and detonate the nuke in order to save the world.

"It will be Harry," Hee-Man whispers to me. "I just know it."

When he sees AJ holding the short straw, I'm pretty sure my friend is going to start crying.

"It cannot be AJ," he argues. "He has a girlfriend back home."

An image of a smiling, gentle-eyed brunette flashes through my mind. *Yeah,* I want to tell him, *just because you've got a girl back home doesn't mean you're going to return safely.*

I know what's coming, but I decide it's best to let Hee-Man experience the drama for himself. Harry takes AJ down to the asteroid's surface, where they get ready to say goodbye.

"His daughter will be so upset." Hee-Man's hardly even talking to me anymore as much as to himself, so I don't reply. I've got a lump in my throat. Somehow knowing that Harry raised AJ changes this entire scene for me, especially the part where Harry forces AJ back into the spaceship with a subdued, "I love you, son."

A minute more of this and both Hee-Man and I are going to be sobbing in one another's arms.

"He did it." Hee-Man's voice is all choked up. "Harry did it. He's going to stay behind. He is sacrificing himself. He is taking AJ's place."

I can't even respond. The minute I try to speak I'm going to cry. Up until now, I've always seen Harry as the tough and hardened alpha male, but now I see him with new eyes. The father figure, full of compassion, sacrificing himself for the son he never had, giving up his own life, not out of duty

107

or heroism or courage but out of love.

AJ's crying, Hee-Man's crying, and now I am too. Harry shouldn't have to do this. He shouldn't have to stay behind and blow himself to bits, but he's going to.

Because he loves AJ.

That, and of course he wants to save the world.

But most of all because he loves AJ. The one he called his son.

I turn off the movie.

"Why did you do that?" Hee-Man doesn't even try to wipe the tears off his cheeks.

"I'm tired," I declare. "I'm done watching for the night."

"What happens?" Hee-Man whines. "Does Harry find a way to survive?"

"No," I tell him. "Harry dies."

"He dies?"

"Yeah. He dies." I roll over and face the wall. Why did I ever agree to watch a movie like this? What was I thinking?

"Is it sad?"

I throw my pillow at him. It's a juvenile response but I suppose it's better than rolling over and knocking him out. "Of course it's sad. That's the whole point of the movie."

"But the world is saved?" Hee-Man presses.

I let out my breath. "Yes. Now stop asking me any more

stupid questions. It's a dumb movie, there's nothing realistic about it, and I'm tired. If you want to finish it, watch the rest yourself but find some headphones or something. I want it quiet."

I feel bad for snapping, I really do, but I can't stop myself. My brain's filled with too much chaos and grief. My heart rate's got to be over a hundred right now. My mind's racing, and I want to bury my head into my pillow and scream. Of course, I can't because I threw my pillow at Hee-Man, who's yet to give it back to me.

"I am sorry," he whispers, and I feel the mattress jostle as he gets off my bed. I don't know what he's apologizing for, and I don't care. I'm too busy thinking about it all. Harry, AJ, the little homeless boy whose life I ruined.

I understand the scene on the asteroid. I understand AJ's tears. He didn't want Harry to sacrifice himself. It would be far easier to end his own life than to watch his father figure die in his place. Funny. All these years and I thought the movie was about action and explosions, but really it's about sacrifice.

Sacrifice and love.

The kind of love I've failed to live up to. And here I go again fixating on that homeless boy. I know it's foolish and paternalistic to think that I could have saved him, but I can't help myself. I should have protected him. Isn't that why I went into journalism to begin with? To give the oppressed and the marginalized a voice of their own?

I failed. Just like the astronauts failed on that asteroid. Because of the mess they made, they had to leave one of their men behind.

Force a man to sacrifice himself, to die in someone else's place.

I would do it in a heartbeat. I know I would. If my imprisonment in North Korea could free that little homeless kid in my photo, I'd take whatever punishment I had coming at me. But it doesn't work that way. If I want to atone for my mistakes, if I want to make it all right, I've got to get out of here. Out of North Korea. Imagine what I could do when I'm released, how all that media attention can be turned to the human rights abuses that Pyongyang inflicts on its own citizens on a daily basis?

I can't be Harry. I can't stay here and sacrifice myself out of some noble sense of duty or calling or even love.

I've got to get back home. That's where I can make a difference. That's where I can correct my mistake from so many years ago. I can't give up here. I can't die yet.

I've got to get back home.

CHAPTER 20

That night I dream about Bruce Willis and me together on an asteroid. We're arguing about who will stay behind and become the savior of the world. I jump up with a start right before I blow myself up. Hee-Man's already awake and looking at me sheepishly.

"Did you sleep well?" he asks, and the first wave of mortification sweeps over me when I see his eyes.

He's afraid of me.

"Yeah," I grumble. I know I owe my friend some sort of apology. I was kind of a monster last night, but I don't know how to admit it. "Did you finish the movie?" I ask.

He shakes his head. "I already knew how it was going to end."

I feel bad but what can I say? I'm no good at this, no good at pretending to be happy when I'm imprisoned and about to stand trial for my life. "Well," I begin, "maybe tonight we can finish it." I hope Hee-Man sees the remark for the gesture of good-will it's intended as.

He shakes his head. "I won't be here tonight."

I had no idea my frayed nerves could get even more frazzled. "What do you mean?"

"I'm going home." He can't quite meet my eyes when he says this.

"Why?" I probably sound like a whining toddler, but I don't care.

He still refuses to look at me. "It's time for me to return to my family. I'm sorry."

"What's going to happen to me?" I ask. I hate to sound so selfish, but given my current situation and emotional state, I hope he'll be forgiving.

"You will stand trial."

I stare at him. Isn't there anything else he can say? I'm like Ebenezer Scrooge once again, begging of his ghost, *Speak comfort to me, Jacob.* But apparently, just like Jacob Marley, Hee-Man has no comfort to give.

"It has been a pleasure knowing you," he says with a polite half-bow.

Tell me that doesn't sound like the final farewell given to a man who stood condemned already?

"Please," I begin. I have to make him understand. "Please tell me what's happening." I don't know what else to say. I don't know who else I can trust if not him. "I don't want you to leave," I finally admit.

This time he raises his eyes to mine, eyes that are full of both compassion and worry. I get a sinking feeling in my gut.

"I have no choice," he admits quietly. "My time here is over."

I figure this is probably all he's allowed to say, and I indulge in a few more moments of sorrow before my self-pity turns into anger. Anger at the way I've spent the past several years, prancing around the world like some sort of knight in shining armor, feeling invincible, totally oblivious to the danger I'm subjecting myself and others to. Anger at whoever handed me over to the North Koreans, anger at Hee-Man for abandoning me. Who's going to replace him? I wonder if it's all because of my little temper tantrum over the movie. Did he request this job transfer?

Has he given up on me?

Just last night, I vowed to fight for my freedom, to survive until this whole mess gets sorted out. But how am I supposed to do that if the man I'm closest to in this entire country doesn't even believe in me?

We don't talk any more about Hee-Man's departure, and I don't know if he's taking off this morning or sometime later in the day. When he tells me he's going to get some breakfast, I'm not even sure if I'll see him again. All I know is I'm alone in a room full of monitors I can't see, I'm about to stand trial as a spy, and my only friend is gone.

But not for long. Hee-Man returns less than half an hour later with a few pastries and an announcement. "I have someone for you to meet."

At first, I assume it's Hee-Man's replacement, but when I see the six-foot-tall white man with a blond goatee, I figure I'm wrong.

He holds out his hand. "Eric Swensson," he tells me. "I'm the Swedish Ambassador to North Korea."

I've been waiting for a meeting like this. Since the US has no diplomatic relationships with Pyongyang, it's historically the Swedes who step in to advocate on behalf of Americans unfortunate enough to find themselves in trouble here.

Hee-Man steps out, and again I wonder if this is the last I'll see of my friend. Eric wants to know about my treatment, if I've been subjected to corporal punishment, the works. I know and he knows we're both being monitored, and this feels far more like a dress rehearsal than an actual meeting. I tell him I'm fine, just a little hungry, and he smiles in what I can only guess is sincerity.

"Do you know why you're being held here?" he asks.

I rattle off the crimes I've already confessed to. Spying for the American government. Inciting to overthrow Pyongyang. None of it appears to surprise him. Either he's already familiar with my case or these are pretty standard accusations in Pyongyang.

"I want you to know that the American government is aware of your situation," he says, and I feel a surprising rush of warmth wash over me. They know where I am. I've suspected as much for a while, but having official confirmation brings a welcome sense of relief.

"I also have a package from your grandmother."

I lean forward in my seat. "Grandma Lucy? Is she all right? Is her health holding up?"

Eric gives a little chuckle. "She's fine. We talked by phone a few days ago, and she wants me to personally inform you that she's not stopped praying for you since she heard of your complications here."

I know she means that literally, and again I give in to that welcome wave of relief.

Eric smiles and passes me an envelope. "I already spoke with the North Koreans, and they've agreed you may have this."

I snatch it out of his hands as a starving child might swipe at food. Upon ripping it open, I immediately recognize

Grandma Lucy's flowing cursive and flowery stationary. "She also wanted to make sure you had access to this." Eric takes out a Bible that I recognize. It's Grandma Lucy's own. This leather-bound book has been in so many of my childhood memories. I'm surprised she gave it up. I guess she's really trying to get through to me.

"Would you like a few minutes to write your grandma a letter in return? I have permission for you to send one letter to family back home. It will obviously have to be approved by the North Koreans before it leaves here, but I can bring you a pen and stationary if you want."

It's so much all at once. A letter from home. My grandma's Bible. An ambassador who appears to be invested in securing my freedom.

I nod, indicating that I would like the pen and paper he's offering.

I'd like that very much.

CHAPTER 21

Dear Grandma Lucy,

Thank you for the letter and all the Bible verses. On that note, thanks for your Bible too. I promise to take good care of it since I know how much it means to you. We'll treat this as if I'm borrowing it for a while. How does that sound?

I'm sure you're worried about me, but I want you to know all my physical needs are being met. All those scary things you think might be happening to me here aren't.

I hate to waste precious paper, but I'm only being allowed to write one note, and I have a few messages I'd like to ask you to pass on for me. First of all, my girlfriend. I told you about her before. I'm sure you remember. Well, we're technically not dating anymore. You'll appreciate this — she dumped me because I'm not a Christian — but I know she's worried about me. In fact, I think the two of you should spend some time getting to know one another. It would make me happy to think of you both becoming friends.

You'll love her. I just know it.

117

Tell Alayna not to spend all her days worrying about her favorite big brother. She's used to me being overseas. She should just pretend I'm on a research trip or something. I'm sure Aunt Connie's worrying herself sick too, so please let her know that I'm fine although I'm working up an appetite. When I come home, I expect a big serving of shepherd's pie and a cinnamon roll at least the size of my head. Hopefully larger.

At this point, the Swedish ambassador and I both agree that as a sign of goodwill to the North Koreans, we'd like to keep publicity as much to a minimum as possible. He seems to believe this will turn out favorably at my trial.

Tell all the aunts and uncles and cousins I appreciate their prayers and well-wishes. It's not as bad right now as they probably think it is, and the thing I have to worry about most is getting bored.

Please take care of your own health as well. I couldn't stand the thought of something happening to you while I'm here.

See you soon,

Ian

CHAPTER 22

After the ambassador leaves, Hee-Man does too. This time I'm pretty sure it's for good because he offers to shake my hand, something he's never done before, and all of a sudden I'm reminded of AJ crying as he says goodbye to Harry on that asteroid. I wonder if Hee-Man still has the flash drive and if he's going to finish *Armageddon* when he gets home.

I'm drained after reading my letter from Grandma Lucy and writing my response. As comforting as it is to know I haven't been forgotten by folks back home, it also accentuates how alone I am. I did what I could to keep my letter positive and uplifting. No sense getting everyone worried, but it's exhausting trying to pretend I'm doing just fine when I know I'm not.

I've never been the kind to get overly anxious about things. I'm pretty chill in my normal, day-to-day life. At least I was before I got arrested. Maybe it's a sign of just how privileged I was, but I never woke up and had to worry about when my next meal would be or whether or not I'd end up spending the rest of my life in a dark, dank prison cell.

I'd get absorbed in my work. I could stay awake for twenty hours a day when I was finishing up a project. Over the summer while I was editing my documentary, I probably spent an average of fifteen or sixteen hours a day on it, fueled entirely by caffeine and adrenaline, but even that was the good kind of stress. The excitement of knowing I was creating something that nobody else in the entire world could make.

And now here I am, no Hee-Man to talk to, no bootlegged American films to watch. Apparently even my prosecutor has taken the day off, as it's past noon and I haven't seen Mr. Kim at all. I don't know what's supposed to happen now. Eric the Swede promised to take my letter and make sure it found its way to Grandma Lucy. He told me to keep cooperating with the North Koreans, and he'd be around again to check on me soon, but I don't know if that means I'll see him again at dinner time or in a year.

I've read and reread Grandma Lucy's letter, which is exactly what I expected it to be. A few encouraging words followed by nothing but Bible verses and prayers she's written out for me. It's comforting she cares enough to pray to her invisible God for my well-being. I'm thankful for that much at least.

Thankful I'm not forgotten.

But now with Hee-Man gone, my trial date looming ever nearer, and so much uncertainty ahead of me, I find myself even more homesick. It's so bad I crack open Grandma Lucy's Bible, and I swear I can hear her warbly voice as I browse through the verses. There are so many scribbles in the margins and highlighted passages I don't even know where to start, but eventually I make my way to Psalm 23, reading it over and over.

I know that if I were a good little Christian like Grandma Lucy once thought me to be, the words would fill me with comfort and hope, but all they do is make me feel even more lonely and abandoned. I shut the Bible and tuck it under my pillow, then lay down to stare at the ceiling while I wait to find out what's going to happen to me next.

CHAPTER 23

I've been privileged enough up until now that I never thought much about mental health. Somewhere in the back of my head is the impression that before she was killed by a drunk driver, my mother suffered from postpartum depression. It must have been after Alayna was born, although I also have some sort of recollection of a miscarriage. These memories take on more of a feel of family legend since after Mom died, my dad stopped talking about her. Aside from these latent memories of an almost forgotten childhood, I've spent the majority of my life basically ignoring issues of mental health.

I suppose a psychologist could look at me and diagnose me now as a classic case of depression. It's not like I've got Google here so I can do an online search or anything, but I'm guessing I have nearly all the symptoms.

Sleep trouble? Absolutely, especially after Hee-Man left. I no longer have a roommate at the hotel, although I'm certain every movement continues to be monitored from the outside. When I'm not speaking with my prosecutor, I spend the days asleep, at night suffering such horrible insomnia I think nearly all my other symptoms could be explained away by lack of sleep and nothing else.

Irritability? Tell that to Mr. Kim, who more than once has called guards in to restrain me when my temper reinforces all those stereotypes about redheads. I'm sick and tired of answering the same stupid questions day in and day out.

"If you want to put me on trial," I shout at him, "just do it. Stop messing around with all this blasted paperwork, and just march me before the judge already."

My time to stand before the judge will come soon enough, Mr. Kim assures me before armed guards force me to cool down.

They say that if you're depressed, you lose interest in the things you once did. That's a hard one to gauge, because it's not like there are many entertainment options while I'm stuck in this room with nothing but my grandma's old Bible for company. But even if I were given the chance to go outside, stretch my legs, or watch a bootlegged Hollywood movie, I'm too tired most days to do anything but lay here.

I spend vast chunks of time thinking about absolutely nothing. My mind's completely shut off. That's what worries me the most. In the past, whenever I found the time for daydreams, I'd imagine all the places I planned to visit, all the issues I planned to research, the documentaries I planned to film. I could mentally splice together all my footage of North Korean refugees and visualize how my documentary could play out in the end. I could see the landscape shots I'd pan through while the interviews are running.

Now, there's nothing. If I do think about my work, it's that picture of that homeless boy and nothing else. His eyes, which I always described as haunting, are now haunting me. They're all I can think about. When I do think at all. But like I already said, most of the time my brain's a complete blank. As if the neural circuits have decided to give up on me just like my friend did. I haven't seen Hee-Man since the day I met with the Swedish ambassador. They tell me about three weeks have passed, and still no trial, no letters from home, no friendly face.

Twice they've had someone I can only assume is a doctor check me out. He listens to my lungs and my heart, he peers into my ears and nose, and he jabbers away in Korean to the minders who are assigned to babysit me. I don't know any of their names. I don't care. The only person I speak to directly is my prosecutor, who still comes to sit with me for hours a day going over my confession, getting me ready for my trial. Meanwhile, every single ounce of energy has leaked out of me, and I have no way to refuel. I don't think I'm starving. I get fed at least twice, more often three times a day. It's enough to keep me alive. But apparently either the lack of food or the mental cloud hanging over me is making it so I can hardly get myself out of bed. I spend ten minutes or more psyching myself up just to make my way to the toilet. That's what I've been reduced to in these few weeks.

On a good day, I might prop open Grandma Lucy's Bible, but my eyes can't focus on the words. It takes three or four times as much mental energy as it should to make my way through a single verse, so I rarely bother. I wish Hee-Man were here. I miss him calling me *American,* I miss his questions about Hollywood. I hope he's happy back home with his family, and I wonder if his little girls like the candy he picked up for them.

Days morph into sleepless nights. The doctor visits me again. I don't think he's pleased with my health. Maybe it has something to do with this cough I've developed. I don't know, and I don't care. I'm not even sure anyone here besides my prosecutor speaks English, so I'm left to myself except for those few hours of meetings with Mr. Kim. I've noticed that the stack of papers he brings along with him has gotten shorter, which I hope is a good sign. It's not that I want to stand trial here in Pyongyang. But at least when it's over something will change. Something has to change. I can't go on like this indefinitely, with this uncertainty, this insomnia, this black hole in my mind.

When I was a kid, my sister and I convinced Grandma Lucy and our dad to let us adopt a stray dog who'd started hanging out around the neighborhood. She was the ugliest thing ever, gray and spotted and mangy, but we loved her back to health. Freckles spent three happy years with our family before she started acting tired. Despondent. The vet said cancer. We could operate, but there was no guarantee it'd do anything for her.

My dad made the decision for us to put Freckles down. Alayna and I begged and threw fits, and I even recall staging a hunger strike, but in the end we had to let her go.

That's how I feel now. Like Freckles with no more energy, no more life. Every breath is painful, both emotionally and physically, and I just want someone to come and have mercy on me and put me out of my torment. That's why I'm not scared when Mr. Kim comes in, hands me a suit, and orders me to get dressed. He doesn't even have to tell me why. I didn't know my trial was going to start today, but that's the only way to explain the monkey suit.

I'm so weak he finally calls a minder in to help me clothe

myself. I'm sure a normal, healthy person would feel humiliated, but I'm not even thinking about that. All I'm thinking about is my dad's gentle voice as he holds Alayna and me after we leave the vet's.

It's better this way. She's not hurting any more. Freckles is at peace.

CHAPTER 24

I suppose I spent my life watching too many courtroom dramas because I have vastly different expectations about what my trial will look like. Here I was, expecting the North Korean equivalent of the paparazzi, but if I took the time to count the people in attendance, I probably wouldn't get past a dozen.

The only two attendees I recognize are Mr. Kim and Eric, the Swedish ambassador, who gives me a surprised glance when I walk by. He can't be surprised that I'm here. It's my own trial, after all. The only other explanation is I look as sick as I feel. Well, what does he expect after a month or longer stuck in a Pyongyang hotel room?

The suit Mr. Kim found for me is too short in the legs and baggy in the shoulders. I wonder how much weight I've lost since I've been here. I hardly slept at all last night, and you'd think the adrenaline from standing trial for my life would keep me focused and alert, but Mr. Kim's voice zooms in and out of focus as he addresses the judge.

He's speaking in Korean, but I'm certain what he's saying. I'm a spy, sent here by the CIA to incite resurrection, blah, blah, blah. I've gotten so used to hearing these accusations I could probably do as good a job prosecuting myself as Mr. Kim.

The judge is just as nondescript as everyone else around me, and I have a hard time focusing on his facial features at all. I'm only vaguely aware that I'm swaying in my seat until my lawyer, a man I met about two minutes before the trial started, pushes a glass of water toward me. I feel the stare of the Swedish ambassador while I drink with shaking hands. I can only handle a few sips at a time. I feel like there must be something wrong with my throat, but I'm too exhausted to invest the energy in wondering what it could be.

At one point, I'm ordered to stand before the judge. A young woman materializes by my side to translate. I'm dizzy, and after a few minutes I nearly collapse until my lawyer gets the judge to grant me permission to sit while I answer questions. Thankfully, he keeps them quite simple.

"Is your name Ian McCallister?"

"Yes."

"Are you an American journalist?"

"Yes."

"Is it true you are making a documentary about North

Korean defectors residing illegally in China?"

"Yes."

"Are you a spy?"

I already know that I'm meant to plead guilty. Everyone — my prosecutor, my friend Hee-Man, even the Swedish ambassador — has told me it has to be this way.

I don't think. I just want to get this over with so I can go back to bed. "Yes."

I figure there must be more. I wonder if my brain even blocked some of it out, but the next thing I remember the judge makes me stand up again and reads me my sentence.

"Ian McCallister, because you've pleaded guilty to six counts of espionage, you are charged with attempts to overthrow the North Korean government and are hereby sentenced to eight years of hard labor. Case dismissed."

CHAPTER 25

I wake up to find myself on the floor, Eric Swensson staring down at me.

"Ian? Ian?" He looks concerned. I try to tell him not to worry, but I can't find my voice.

"It's all right," he tells me when he sees that I'm awake. "It was bound to happen this way. It's what we were expecting."

I'm having a hard time stringing his words together into coherent meanings.

"The sentence had to come first," he explains. "Now we'll get the Americans involved. The North Koreans have put their chips on the table. It's time for the bargaining to begin."

His tone is reassuring. I expect he's trying to comfort me, which is odd because I don't remember feeling scared or worried or in need of assurance to begin with.

Eric reaches out and feels my forehead. "Has he been given any medical attention?" he demands, and I wonder why if Eric's supposed to be watching out for my welfare he doesn't know about the doctor visits already.

I just need to take a little rest. I need to make all the noise go away. I'm not trying to be rude, but I've got to tune the Swedish guy out. I shut my eyes again and listen with mild curiosity as Eric's voice fades to nothing.

I had no idea I could do that.

Next thing I know, I'm blissfully ignorant of everything going on around me, and all I can hear is the echo of my father's voice as he drives me and my sister home while we cry over the ugly mutt we had to put down.

Freckles is at peace.

CHAPTER 26

Over the next few days, I'm vaguely aware of my surroundings, just conscious enough to know that I'm not doing too hot. I sleep. I wake up to see random faces encouraging me to eat or drink, men with frowns asking how I feel or women with scared faces checking my vitals. I don't hurt. I'm not tired or hungry. Why don't they just let me rest? If anyone asks me a question beyond my name, my head splits when I think about the answer.

The sun is shining in through my window, nearly blinding me as I try to blink it back off.

"Good morning." The voice that greets me is familiar but feels out of place here.

Hee-Man?

He smiles and pulls his chair a little closer to my bedside. "Are you thirsty?" He holds a straw toward me, and I take a sip of what tastes like rusty water.

"What are you doing here?" I can tell my words aren't coming out clearly, but he must have anticipated my

133

question because he answers, "I came to check on you, American. What did you expect?"

I don't tell him that I expected him to dessert me forever, that I expected him to go back home to his pretty wife and two little daughters and forget all about me.

He reaches into his back pocket. "By the way, my daughter drew this picture for you."

I force my eyes to focus on the crude pencil sketch he holds up. I gather the tall man with the huge nose must be me while the one half his size is Hee-Man.

"She is a talented artist, isn't she?"

I still don't know if my friend understands sarcasm, so I decide to play it safe and assume he's speaking in earnest. "Yes, she's wonderful," I agree. "One day her paintings will be all over Pyongyang."

"No, my friend." Hee-Man smiles at me. "You mean all over the world."

He stands up. I'm still too out of it to understand what he's doing at my bedside or how long he's been here. I'm not even sure where *here* is, although I've put enough pieces together to assume I'm at some sort of hospital. What I'm being treated for is anybody's guess.

I grab Hee-Man's hand before he can leave. "Am I sick?"

He frowns at me. "I should get the doctor."

It's nothing like an American hospital. No monitors beeping at me, no machines to tell the nurses what my heart rate is, how my blood pressure's doing, if my body's getting enough oxygen or not. A woman comes in following Hee-Man and shoves a mercury thermometer under my tongue. I haven't seen one of these things in decades and decide I'm lucky she's shoved it in my mouth and not in any of my other orifices.

She stands frowning, and Hee-Man seems to share her concern. I want to ask what's wrong, but of course I can't talk with this thing beneath my tongue.

The woman pulls the thermometer out, gives it a few shakes, then shoves it under my tongue again. This process is repeated until she finally seems convinced it's had enough time to rise and hurries out of the room.

"How bad is it?" I ask Hee-Man.

"Over 104."

"How long have I been here?"

He sighs. "This is your fifth day in the hospital."

I don't know what to say. I have only the vaguest of memories of the past few days, but I can recall the trial. I remember hearing my sentence. Eight years of hard labor for my crimes against the state. In a way, it's more lenient than what it may have been. If Mr. Kim got his way, I'm sure I would have gotten a life sentence or the death penalty. I want to ask Hee-Man again why he's here, but I'm afraid to waste the energy just to get the same answer as before: *to check on you, American.*

Thankfully, my friend doesn't wait for me to carry the conversation. "Your story has caused quite a stir in the world news."

I don't know if that's supposed to make me feel better or not.

"A lot of people in Pyongyang are talking about how lucky you are. It could have been much worse. The ruling was very gracious."

I know this much is true, and I suppose I should feel thankful. I'm surprised at how numb I am, both emotionally and physically, and I wonder if my psyche is shutting down alongside my body.

"What's wrong with me?" I ask and then decide I better rephrase the question. "I mean, what am I sick with?"

Hee-Man's expression remains gentle. "The doctor thinks it is pneumonia. Maybe stress related."

I've never been to medical school, but I'm pretty sure that healthy men my age don't get pneumonia simply from being stressed. But maybe it's different when you're kept on near-starvation rations in a country whose healthcare looks and feels like what you'd expect from a MASH unit in the Korean War.

Even though I'm no doctor, I'm grateful that pneumonia is one of those diseases that can be treated readily. Thank God for antibiotics, right? And even though North Korea's healthcare system may be stunted compared to that of other nations, I know enough to expect a round of treatments and then I'll be strong and healthy again.

Strong and healthy enough to join the labor camps. Right? Isn't that what this is all about? Making me whole so they can break me down? Well, I won't worry about it right now. One day at a time, all that junk. If my little run-in with pneumonia means I've earned a week or two off to recoup after the trial, I'll take it. Maybe Grandma Lucy's over there in Washington right now praying for my guards to show me some leniency. Maybe she heard about my hard labor sentence and has been praying against it. Well, keep on praying, Grandma Lucy. I need all the help I can get.

Hee-Man wants me to drink another sip of rust-water, so I oblige him. As I lean back on my pillow, I sense the slightest hint of emotion creeping over me. It feels unpracticed, as if my brain isn't used to processing anything other than the autonomic functions keeping me alive, but I'm self-aware enough that I can give this feeling a name.

Thankful.

I'm not in the labor camps. Yet. Hee-Man's here, and from what I can tell, the people who are taking care of me sincerely want to see me recover.

I've been in North Korea now for what's got to be a month and a half or so, and the worst things that have happened to me are being told I'm a bad prisoner, having to stand in a corner, and catching pneumonia.

Think about how much worse it could have been, and I suppose this wave of gratitude makes sense.

Maybe Grandma Lucy's prayers are working after all.

Or maybe I'm delirious from fever.

Either way, I'm glad that at this exact moment I'm not tired, hungry, or afraid. I don't have to answer to any interrogator or stand before any judge or plead for my freedom. I just have to lie down in this hospital bed while Hee-Man chats away beside me. I have to give my body and mind a chance to heal, and that's all I'm going to focus on right now.

I make a mental note that when I get home I'm going to tell Grandma Lucy all about the way I learned how to finally take one of her Bible verses and put it into practice. I can hear her craggy voice quoting it in my ear.

Do not worry about tomorrow, for tomorrow will worry about itself. Each day has enough troubles of its own.

CHAPTER 27

Hee-Man spends the next several days in the hospital by my side. He's the translator between me and the doctor and nurses, and he's my comic relief and guarantee against boredom.

"I'm teaching my oldest daughter some English phrases. She already knows how to say *Hello, American* without any accent at all."

I'm not sure if it's dangerous for Hee-Man to teach his daughter English, if that sort of thing is encouraged in a country like this, or if the higher-ups don't care one way or the other. But I figure Hee-Man's had an entire lifetime to learn the ins and outs of his nation's idiosyncrasies, so if he thinks it's something to be proud of, who am I to tell him otherwise?

"Now," Hee-Man demands one afternoon, "you have to teach me a few American jokes I can go home and tell my girls."

Jokes? What's he expect? That I have a thirty-minute

standup routine in my back pocket?

I try to think of a joke that could translate well, but I'm stuck at *What's black and white and red all over?*

We go back and forth with a few riddles I remember from my childhood, but they're about as successful as Jimmy Fallon would be doing a private comedy act for the Queen of England.

The Korean ones Hee-Man tells me fare just as poorly.

"What does a vampire drink for breakfast?" Hee-Man is so tickled by the upcoming punchline, his face is red from trying to stifle his guffaw.

"I don't know," I answer. "What?"

Hee-Man leans forward and bellows, "A bloody nose," spraying saliva everywhere as he lets out the laugh he's been holding in.

I figure that we've found ourselves in the smack middle of a cultural and linguistical impasse, and I give up with riddles for the day.

My doc doesn't have the same English language skills but his curiosity about America is just as strong as Hee-Man's. The times we manage to communicate, he asks me about hamburgers of all things. I'm exhausted just trying to keep up the most basic of conversations with him.

A week passes, and Hee-Man tells me once more that it's

time for him to go home to his family. I'm more used to this coming and going by now, so I don't bother with a long, drawn-out goodbye and I don't allow myself to fall into despondency when he leaves. I tell myself that Hee-Man's the kind of friend who'll keep popping back into my life when I need him. I have to believe that or I couldn't stand to watch him walk out that door.

Well, Grandma Lucy, I can pretty much guarantee you were the one to think of praying for me to find a friend here, so now that Hee-Man's gone back home, what's your God going to do? I sit and wait, and it's not twenty minutes after Hee-Man takes off that I hear a yip coming from outside. I have to turn my head almost 180 degrees just to look out the window, but there's a mangy dog in the courtyard, even uglier and scrawnier than Freckles was, and he's got his paws against the glass and is barking at me happily.

When the nurse comes by later, I ask her if she could slide my bed over a foot, and that gives me a better view. The hospital complex has a small courtyard in the middle. That's where my new friend is happily playing. Every so often I watch as nurses or orderlies stroll by. He's always careful to leave them alone, and they seem content enough to ignore his existence. Maybe he's lonely too, and that's why he's here at my window.

I go to sleep and dream about Freckles before she got cancer. When I wake up in the morning, I can still feel the spot on my cheek where she was so happily licking away, but the dingy surroundings immediately remind me that the poor mutt's been dead for two decades and I might end up that way too if Doc can't get this pneumonia under control.

I wheeze with every breath I take, and there are hours out of each day where I actively have to concentrate on my breathing or I'm pretty certain my lungs would decide to stop working altogether. I've never been sickly, I've never had asthma, and I'm thankful for this emotional numbness that's protecting me because I doubt I've been in this much pain in my entire life. I don't know if it's Doc's meds that are taking the edge off or some fortunate psychological phenomenon that allows me to go through the bulk of my days in some sort of emotional stupor.

Unfortunately, that same psychological protection that's keeping the worst of despair at bay also means I'm not experiencing things like happiness or gratitude in the same way a healthy person would. That's why it feels so strange to wake up after dreaming about Freckles. I remember actually laughing and wonder if that was all in my head or if I was giggling in my sleep as well.

I steel myself against the crashing disappointment that overwhelms me when I realize Freckles is just as dead now as she was when my dad drove my sister and me home from the vet's. That's when I hear the barking again.

I glance out the window and see my mangy friend. I reach my hand out, but I'm not quite close enough to touch the glass. The dog puts its paws up on the glass and barks even more enthusiastically. That afternoon I ask Doc if he thinks I'm strong enough to go for a little walk in the fresh air. He doesn't trust my legs (and the first time I try to support my weight I understand why), but he tells me that when a nurse is free he'll see if she can wheel me out.

"I think I'd just like to sit out in the courtyard for a little bit." Even as I say the words and point out the window to make sure Doc understands, I'm looking for my canine friend. Where'd he go?

It's evening before either Doc remembers what we talked about or he finds a nurse who isn't too busy to help. The woman who comes to wheel me outside is probably a foot shorter than I am, but she easily transfers me into the wheelchair. I'm glad there's no mirrors in here. I'd hate to see how pathetic I look and how much weight I've lost.

To get to the courtyard area, we have to pass through a hallway with long window panes along the side. Rusty (yes,

I've named him) runs along from the outside, barking the entire time. I think he knows we're about to have a proper meeting. None of this putting our paws up against the window to say hi anymore.

Once outside, I ask the nurse to leave my wheelchair here for a while, even though I'm pretty sure that once Hee-Man left, Doc became the only English speaker in the complex. Rusty's already got his front paws on my lap, wagging his tail so enthusiastically I'm paranoid he's about to pee on my leg. Thankfully, he controls his bladder, and the laughter he elicits when he starts licking my face as if I were covered in peanut butter is better medicine than anything Doc or the finest physicians in America could offer.

I think the staff here must have forgotten about me because the sun's already set before someone thinks to come out and wheel me back inside. I'm shivering from the cold, but I'm sad to leave my friend.

"See you tomorrow," I tell Rusty, giving his ears a final scratch. He looks at me with such understanding eyes I'm convinced he comprehends my English better than anyone else in this hospital. "Have a good night, pal."

Rusty wags his tail then trots off to follow me in the windows as my nurse wheels me back to my room.

That night, I sleep peacefully, and when I wake up, the

first thing I do is look out my window to find two paws pressed up against the glass and a black nose making patterns in the frost that condensed onto the window overnight.

CHAPTER 28

The following days pass in very much the same way. Sometime around lunch I ask to be wheeled out to the courtyard, and I spend the next several hours with my dog. I have to brace myself because Rusty licks my face so enthusiastically I can hardly breath. His breath is gross, but I'm so happy to have a friend I don't care.

Through sign language, I'm able to ask one of the nurses for a comb. It's a terrible tool to use to groom a matted, mangy dog, but I do what I can and hope that Rusty understands I'm not actively trying to torture him. It takes longer than I expect — a total of about six hours spread out over three afternoons — until his coat is tangle-free and shining. I even manage to make a ball for him out of some old cloth bandages my nurse was about to throw out. What I didn't realize until now is that not all dogs are born with the innate ability to play fetch, and Rusty thinks I've brought him a chew toy. I'm pretty sure that over the course of our next two outings together, he ingests the majority of the bandage. I hope it doesn't upset his stomach.

146

Doc seems happy with my progress, but whenever I tell him I'm starting to feel better, he shakes his head at me and scowls. I don't understand this. Not at first. Then one morning he takes my temperature and it's back to normal. I can inhale without feeling like there's glass lodged into my lungs. I smile and tell Doc I'm a new man, but he shushes me.

"If you're not sick, it's to the camps."

I consider myself a complete idiot not to have realized sooner that Doc's doing me a massive favor. When officers from the state come to check on me every few days, Doc makes sure I'm hooked up to the IV even though my antibiotic treatment's over now, and from what I can tell, it's only saline in those bags. He frowns a lot and clucks his tongue each time he checks my vitals. I wonder if seeds of rebellion begin like this, with small acts of kindness shown to enemies of the regime. Maybe by prolonging my hospital stay, Doc's well on his way to starting the revolution that will help the North Koreans truly achieve their freedom.

These are the thoughts running through my head when the men from the state come by yet again, and yet again Doc appears to fret and fawn over me far more zealously than he does when they're gone. Once I realize what's happening, I even play along, acting weaker and hoping to appear even more pathetic when they're around.

Who would have known that playing hooky when I was in sixth grade would teach me such important survival skills? Only the stakes are far higher than a failed test or a trip to the principal's office.

One morning Doc comes in, looking so distraught I'm afraid he's going to tell me he found a lung tumor and I only have hours to live.

"I talked with the National Security Agency," he says. I don't even know exactly which government division that is, but I know they're at least one of the key players in my case. "They come for you at noon."

I wish Hee-Man were here to translate. I think I understand what Doc's saying. In fact, I know that I do, but my brain wants to convince me it's a mistake.

I tell Doc I'd like one last visit to the courtyard. Rusty's nose is already pressed up against the pane, and he's fogging it up with his doggy breath.

Doc sighs and nods. I don't even need the wheelchair anymore. All pretense is over. He allows me to walk myself to the courtyard. Rusty's enthusiastic jumping quickly turns into whines. He knows. Don't ask me how, but the ugly mutt knows this is goodbye. That's why he's whimpering into my shoulder as I wet his perfectly groomed (but still ugly as all get out) fur with my tears.

"Thank you, buddy," I whisper to him. "I'll never forget you."

He whimpers weakly in response and gives me one last lick on the lips. I'm already aching with loneliness at the thought of leaving him here, and I can't be bothered to wipe the dog drool off my mouth.

A few hours later, I'm calm and collected when two men from the NSA come to transport me to prison camp.

My hard labor sentence has just begun.

CHAPTER 29

I'm led out of the hospital toward a black SUV. I don't know if I'm imagining things or not, but I think I can hear Rusty barking in the distance.

"Thank you, buddy, for everything" I whisper as a man in uniform shoves me into the backseat.

I don't know why, but as we start our drive, I think about the road trips we used to take, Dad, my sister Alayna, and me. There was this Christian camp on the Oregon coast that hosted a family retreat every fourth of July. My happy memories quickly turn maudlin as I think about my future. Eight Independence Days trapped here in North Korea. Somehow I doubt there'll be fireworks.

Those summer camps were always exciting. Most of the time, Dad was too busy with work to be bothered with things like vacations. Even the road trip was nice. Maybe that's because I was the oldest and always got to sit in front while Alayna was stuck playing with her dolls and crossword puzzles in the back. I have no idea how long this trip's supposed to take, but I'm squished between two guards, and from what I can gather I'm the only one in the car who speaks a word of English. Through a lot of snappy phrases, sign language, and eventually some pushing and shoving, I understand I need to bury my head in my lap. You can guess how comfortable that is.

I guess it's just as well, though. This way they can't see the tears streaking down my face. I'm not too macho to admit I'm crying. What does embarrass me, though, is I'm not mourning my loss of freedom. I'm not scared of whatever torment lies ahead of me.

I'm crying because I miss Rusty, and I worry that now I'm gone there won't be anyone to take care of him.

My tears are dry but my back's cramped up when one of the guards prods me in the side and snaps something at me. I take it to mean I don't have to bend over any more, and when I glance out the window, I see we're out of the city. Makes sense. I guess a nation like North Korea wouldn't put their labor camps right in the heart of one of the only places where tourists are allowed to visit. Something about the landscape, the quietness of it all, again reminds me of those drives to the Oregon Coast.

I'm feeling bad that I haven't kept in touch with Alayna like I should have been over the past few years. We were close as kids, at least I'm told we were. Honestly my memories are hazy up until junior high, and by that point in our lives all I can remember is her being a stereotypical preteen, lounging around malls, tying up the phone for hours on end while she spread the junior-high gossip.

I only graduated a year before she did, but by that point we moved around in completely separate spheres. I thought we were both content with this arrangement, but she's since told me that all through our high school years she felt like she was living in my shadow. Which is funny, because from the way I remember it, she was the popular, straight-A cheerleader, and I was the weird journalism geek who always befriended the nerds and loners and protected them from bullies.

It's all a matter of perspective, I guess, isn't it?

Alayna's doing well. She lives out in Alaska with her husband and their three boys. I don't know my nephews nearly as well as I should. For all the world traveling I've done, it's not like Anchorage is that far of a stretch. You don't even need a passport to hop on a plane and fly up there.

I hope Grandma Lucy's been passing my letters on to my sister. I hope Alayna's not too worried about me. It's funny how my brain's doing this. Focusing on other things, other people, other problems. It's like I can't handle the fact that

I'm about to be handed a prison uniform and forced to endure hard labor at a modern-day gulag. So I'm thinking about my sister. Or if not her, I'm thinking about my girlfriend, the one who really isn't, and the way she encouraged me all summer through those relentless hours of video editing. When my corneas grew so dry it felt like my eyelids were lined with sandpaper, she was my encouragement, my enthusiasm, my muse.

And even though she broke up with me, I wonder if she knows how much I think about her.

How much I care about her.

How deeply I love her, and how much I regret not telling her the truth. I always assumed she knew, but now I'll never know for sure.

An eight-year sentence? She could be married with more children than Alayna by the time I see her again.

When I'm not thinking about her, I'm fixating on Rusty, worrying that his coat will get just as matted and tangled as it was when I met him. Or I'm worried that my sister won't be able to focus on her family or her kids because she's too scared about what will happen to me.

It's strange. In high school, I was still fairly religious. I mean, I went to church whenever Grandma Lucy told me to (in other words, several times a week), and I didn't argue or complain. Alayna was the one who rolled her eyes at it, like she was too good for church and the lowlifes who went to the Orchard Grove youth group were going to tarnish her pristine reputation. Now she's married to a pastor, and my nephews attend even more church functions than I did when I was their age. And here I am, the atheist-agnostic who's been praying every day since my arrest.

They let me keep Grandma Lucy's Bible when I was at the hospital, but I had to turn it in to the Swedish ambassador before they brought me here. I hope it finds its way back to Grandma Lucy, and now I wish I'd read it more. It's funny how even in my captivity I'm taking things for granted until they're stripped away from me. As the view out the SUV window grows more rural, bringing me closer to my fate, I wonder how many nights I'll lay awake wishing I had Grandma Lucy's worn copy of Scripture with me. Wishing I would have read it more when I actually had the chance.

Well, it's too late for that now. This is my future.

I hope I'm ready for it, but as I find myself wincing in pain and fear each time the tires roll over a pothole in the road, I have a feeling I'm not.

Not ready for it at all.

CHAPTER 30

I'm shaking by the time I get out of the SUV, and I have to pee too, so I hope there's an outhouse or something they'll let me use. I find myself wishing for the mental numbness that characterized so much of my stay in Doc's hospital, but unfortunately my body thinks I need to be completely alert right now. My mind has never been clearer.

Or more terrified.

The officers seated beside me must sense how scared I am as I shake and quiver beside them. I have no idea what they're saying, but my guess from their laughter is that they're making fun of me. It's like I'm in elementary school, standing up to yet another bully who has decided he wants to beat up my best friend, only now the stakes aren't skinned knees and a possible trip to the principal's. I find myself wishing I'd never gone through that phase in high school, reading every memoir from Holocaust survivors I could get my hands on. If my fate is going to be on par with what they might have suffered, I certainly don't want to know about it ahead of time. I wish I could be blissfully ignorant.

We roll past watch towers and security checkpoints, and I clench my jaw shut to keep my teeth from rattling. If there is a God, I have no idea how he expects me to endure what's waiting for me, and I hate the fact that I feel so surprised. *This sort of stuff doesn't happen to people like me.* It's the result of privileged thinking. The fact of the matter is this *stuff* happens to hundreds of thousands of people all across the world. Did I truly think that since I'm white and American, I was immune from this type of suffering?

To my shame, that's exactly how I feel. I wonder if being sent to a prison camp is easier if you grow up under a harsh dictatorship, if every day of your life you know that this is the fate that might overtake you if you or anyone in your immediate family falls out of favor with the Party, but that's probably privileged thinking too. Unendurable suffering is unendurable no matter what kind of background you come from. I'm just glad I'm not carrying around any government secrets or sensitive information. In the emotional state I'm in, all I'd need is for an interrogator to sneeze at me and I'd tell him anything he wanted to know and probably wet myself before I finished.

I've read in books and memoirs about how when

someone goes through an intensely traumatic experience, they feel like they're watching it happen to someone else. I wish I could experience that out of body state right now. I wish to God I could. I wonder if that means I'm actually less of an atheist than I once thought I was. Grandma Lucy's fond of reminding me and anyone else who will listen that trials in life will either bring you closer to the Lord or farther away from him. In fact, I know with certainty that she attributes my turning away from the God of the Bible on the fact that my mother died when I was so young. She persists in this belief even though I spent over a decade and a half after Mom's death going to church and believing everything she did before the blinders finally fell off during my first year of college. Maybe she's so upset at having her grandson turn away from the faith that she had to come up with some sort of excuse or she'll blame herself for my de-conversion.

I'd love someone else to blame for my present situation. I'd love to be angry at God for sending me here or at the American government for failing to secure my rescue or at the Swedish ambassador for not doing more to advocate for my release. But there's not a single person I can blame. I've never bought into the whole noble philosophy that all suffering serves some sort of grand purpose. Sometimes terrible things happen, and there's no reason for it, no redemption, no scapegoat worthy to take the blame. Children get caught in the crosshairs of war. Dads die in freak accidents. Drunk drivers swerve and kill devoted moms every single day. Anyone who thinks they are immune from suffering is deluded, and I have to admit that I happily lived in this delusion for the bulk of my adult life.

Looking back, I've had it extremely easy. Sure, I felt sorry for myself that I had to grow up without a mother, but she died when I was so young that I don't remember actively missing her. Dad's death was hard, but we had a full year to see it coming, and he died at peace with his family and those around him after living a fulfilled, albeit somewhat shorter than expected, life.

As far as my own personal history goes, the past few weeks are the only time I've ever been hospitalized. I've never fallen prey before to any major crime, illness, or natural disaster. I've never been a victim of racism, poverty, or any other form of oppression. That's one thing that's got me so scared right now. I haven't had any life experiences that could come close to preparing me for the trials I know lie ahead.

Trials I know I'm not going to be able to endure.

Trials that could kill me if I let them.

We roll past a last checkpoint and into a complex surrounded by barbed wire with watchtowers positioned every hundred feet or so. The driver stops the SUV in front of a square building, and I'm immediately prodded on both sides by my captors. It's time for me to get out of the car. It's time for me to start the first day of hard labor.

CHAPTER 31

I don't know exactly what I was expecting would happen once I got out of the SUV. I guess I figured that since I'm to spend my time here in a hard labor camp that I be handed some sort of pickax or shovel and set to work straight away. I failed to take into account that every country — dictatorship or not — has its own version of bureaucracy. Since no one around me speaks English, I'm left to guess at what's being discussed. This is better than being sent to some work factory, I tell myself, but it does little to assuage my nerves and absolutely nothing to relieve the pressure in my bladder. There are half a dozen people apparently shouting and arguing about my case, and I hate the fact that I'm too scared to stand up and let someone know I need to pee. Doc may have pulled me through my first and hopefully only experience with pneumonia, but I'm just as likely to die of a bladder infection here if I can't find some place to relieve myself soon.

My mind is racing over everything I learned and

researched about North Korean prison camps. One of the defectors I interviewed for my documentary escaped from a place like this. There was some kind of prison riot, a distraction. While the guards weren't looking, he made his way through the barbed wire, into the mountainous wilderness that separated him from the Chinese border. He was living as a naturalized South Korean citizen when I found him, and he was much more open about his escape through the mountains than he was about his time in prison camp. I wonder if I would have the strength to do what he did if the chance should present itself to me to escape.

After what feels like hours, the waiting made even more unbearable by the fact that I still haven't found a place to urinate, the driver and two guards who were so kind as to escort me here leave without a word of parting or a backward glance. Two other workers shuffle off to the back where I can only assume there are more offices for the camp administration, and I'm left alone with a little mustached clerk who stares at me with wide eyes. I'm reminded of the time I freaked out after finding a raccoon trapped in our trashcan. "Remember," my dad calmly stated, "He's more afraid of you than you are of him."

I probably wouldn't be wrong to assume that I'm the first American this clerk has ever seen up close and in person. I wonder what kind of lies he grew up believing about me and my people. He tosses me a gray uniform and gestures impatiently to tell me that I'm expected to change here. I hate myself for traveling so often to Asia yet never learning the Korean word for *bathroom*.

The prison pants were obviously meant for someone much shorter than I am, but they fit fine around the waist. Same thing with the shirt. The man snatches my discarded clothes, the last possessions I can call my own, and I know for certain I'll never see them again.

A picture of Rusty back at the hospital courtyard flashes through my mind, and I picture myself burying my head into his warm fur and petting him while his tail happily thumps the ground. The memory gives me a small burst of courage. The clerk is telling me something, and when he opens the door leading outside, I know I'm meant to follow. I may be the only American condemned to hard labor at this camp, but I'm certainly not the only human being here. Praying that somehow I might be able to overcome the cultural and language barriers that have kept me so isolated and alone, I follow the man wherever it is he might be leading me.

CHAPTER 32

The sun's almost set by the time I step foot out of their little administration building, and the gravity of my situation starts to sink in. I know nobody here. I don't speak any of the language because, just like the stupid and brash American I am, I never expected to find myself in a part of the world where I couldn't get by with plain old English.

I've seen today's date multiple times on multiple sheets of formal paperwork I've had to sign. I know I've missed Grandma Lucy's birthday. Missed it by several weeks. Leaves will be changing back home. If the chill that's already seeped into the evening air is any indication, winter will be upon us soon. My first of eight winters here in a hard labor camp.

My prison uniform smells like mold. There is no way I'll ever get used to any of this. As I follow the clerk, some sort of survival instinct kicks in and tells me it would be a bad idea to make eye contact with any of the prisoners or guards we pass, even though everyone who sees me stares. It's not my red hair that incites this reaction anymore. That was all shaved off as of about fifteen minutes ago. But I'm still most obviously foreign, most obviously American, and I know enough about the North Korean propaganda machines to assume that the people who see me must find me a terrifying sight.

I've never felt so alone or abandoned, forgotten by my country, my government. I remember enough from my church upbringing to know the Bible teaches that God is everywhere, but none of my Sunday school teachers could fathom a place like this, let alone expect to serve here as a prisoner.

We pass a group of children, somber and serious. I scan their faces. Would I recognize the little homeless boy from my photograph if I saw him again? My chest is squeezing, and it's hard to take in a breath. Is this the pneumonia again or something else?

My soul aches for a friendly word, a kindly glance, some sort of humane gesture in the sea of bleak oppression, but everyone who sees me gawks with hatred and fear mixed together, and I'm alone.

I'm led into a cement fortress and follow the clerk to a desk. More talking. More words in Korean that I can't understand. A guard stands and shouts something at me. The clerk takes his leave, and now I'm following another nameless man in this nameless prison through a seemingly endless labyrinth. I don't know if this building is a dorm or the factory where they're going to put me to work or a torture cell where I'll face more interrogations. I don't know anything. As vehemently as I've opposed the current Washington administration, I find myself trying to send the President himself some sort of telepathic message. *I'm here. I need help. Please come rescue me.* I never followed through with my international relations degree, but I know enough politics to understand that if diplomacy could have saved me, I'd be back in the States by now. Back with Grandma Lucy, wishing her a happy birthday, helping my Aunt Connie milk her goats, sitting before an endless supply of cinnamon rolls and fattening pastries.

Instead I'm here. The guard barks at me, I vow to never travel to a foreign country again without spending at least a few weeks learning some basic vocabulary, and then I'm led into a cell. There is no bed. No wash area. In the corner stands an overflowing waste bucket, the only furniture in my new home.

The guard gives me one last snappy command — he may as well be reminding me to brush and floss my teeth for all I can understand him — and then my cell door closes shut with a deafening thud.

CHAPTER 33

There is no light in my new room. No windows. The door is completely solid, no metal bars to show me what's happening in the corridor outside. It's as if the universe has shrunk to an eight foot by eight foot cage, and here's where I'll remain, forgotten until my death.

I wish I had something with me that was mine. Grandma Lucy's letter or even my old pair of jeans, saggy as they'd be by this point. I knew that I'd regret not reading Grandma Lucy's Bible when I had it with me in Pyongyang.

I've been sitting all day, but my legs are too weak to hold me up. Every time I try to stand, I sink back down to the cold floor, leaning my back against the concrete wall. There's nothing you can tell yourself, no prayer or curse or mantra appropriate for this kind of situation. I know millions have experienced injustice comparable to this or worse throughout history, but no matter how much you study human rights abuses, you're still never going to be prepared for the day when you yourself become the nameless victim.

166

The shaved man in prison clothes shivering in your cell. The homesick American who only wants to wish his grandma a belated happy birthday. I'm no spy. If my captors had bothered to do their research, they could see the trail I left to prove how much of a pacifist I am.

But none of that matters now. My identity — Ian, the redheaded journalist from Cambridge — is totally irrelevant here. None of it matters. My degrees, my career successes to date, nothing. Pyongyang would still find some way to punish me for being the dangerous criminal they say I am.

I bury my forehead on my knees. I've always liked the idea of meditation and mindfulness, but I never made time to practice any of those skills. I just need something to focus on. When I was growing up, Grandma Lucy would give me magazines and newsletters about persecuted Christians around the world. The stories were always the same, triumph in the face of suffering, tales of Christians who went to their deaths with singing or led their captors to Christ while enduring the most gruesome of torments.

If Grandma Lucy were here, she'd be just like those victorious believers I used to read about. She'd be praying and singing and witnessing to everyone around her. I choke on a sob, barely able to swallow it down.

I miss her so much.

Tomorrow I'll have to find a way to step out of this self-pity that's threatening to drown me. Tomorrow I'll have to make myself a promise to develop the mental discipline it's going to take to maintain my humanity in spite of my surroundings. But tonight, until sleep overtakes me or a guard starts to beat me, I'm going to allow myself this chance to mourn everything that I've lost. Freedom, family, identity, sense of home. None of these belong to me anymore. Now I'm the prisoner. Ian, the criminal. Ian, the orphan from America, whose own country has forgotten to send anyone to swoop in and save me from my distress.

Tomorrow the sun will rise, and I'll somehow manage to find the strength to face a brand new day. But tonight I can do nothing but lie here, broken, terrified, and horribly alone.

CHAPTER 34

It's morning, and the electric lightbulb in my cell flickers in a valiant attempt to turn on. Every muscle in my body is sore. I'm fairly certain that even after I got to sleep, I spent the entire night shivering. If this is what it's like in the fall, what will happen to me once winter settles in?

Only a moment after the light wakes me up, a man walks into my room. "Prisoner 249." The fact that he is speaking to me in English negates any disappointment I might otherwise have felt to discover that my identity has been reduced here to a mere number.

I jumped to my feet. "Yes, sir."

"I trust you found our accommodations comfortable and convenient?" he asks. It's yet another one of those cultural impasses where I'm left unable to detect sarcasm with any hint of accuracy.

I assume that the less I say, the safer I'll be. "It was fine. Thanks."

He scowls. "You will address me as sir."

169

It's too early in the morning, and my body's too exhausted to argue. "Yes, sir. Sorry." I don't want to overdo it, but I don't want to make him any angrier than he already is, so I tack on one last "sir" at the end for good measure.

He appears placated enough for now. "You will follow me to our briefing room."

My emotions are so numb, I'm immune to any hint of hope, but logically I recognize that following him to a briefing room is better than following him to a labor mine or interrogation chamber. As we walk down the dimly lit hallway, I cast glances to the right and left, trying to figure out the layout of the cells, curious to see what other kind of prisoners they keep detained down here.

We go up a flight of stairs, and now that we're no longer underground, I see the sun appearing over the horizon. I've never wanted a Starbucks caramel macchiato more in my life than I do right now. Extra whipped cream. Extra hot.

The briefing room is just what it sounds like, with a number of mismatched chairs surrounding a conference table. The room could easily accommodate a dozen, but this morning it's just me, the English-speaking guard, and the one man in all of North Korea I'm truly happy to see.

"Hee-man!" I want to run up and throw my arms around him, a strange urge given that I'm not the most overly affectionate guy you'll meet, but the scowl on his face and the quick shake of his head force me to be far more reserved, and I take my seat.

My heart is pounding, and I've gotten so skinny I wouldn't be surprised if Hee-Man could actually see it pounding beneath this threadbare prison shirt. For a moment, I'm faced with the gripping fear that Hee-Man has been arrested, that I now have yet another individual's ruined life on my conscience, but he's dressed in his civilian clothes, and I can only assume he's here for his job. Which apparently means checking up on me every so often no matter where I find myself in this godforsaken country.

The guard takes his seat at the middle of the table, and Hee-Man and I exchange awkward glances from the two far ends. I think about how happy my friend was for the chance to see the sights and the sounds in Pyongyang, and I can only guess that following me to a prison camp is a far less desirable assignment than his previous one. I want to ask how his daughters are. I want to find out if he's watched any more American films. I want to cling to him and tell him how happy I am to see him, but neither of us speak.

The guard clears his throat. "Prisoner 249, I assume you already know what charges have brought you here."

I do my best to look truly repentant, even though I'm so

happy to see a familiar and friendly face I could jump up and kiss Hee-Man right here.

"Your situation is quite delicate," the guard explains. "You've been assigned to hard labor at Camp 22, but of course we can't have you mingling with the other prisoners and corrupting them with your Western propaganda."

I don't know how to respond to this or if I am even expected to, and I glance toward Hee-Man who is expertly avoiding my gaze.

"Seeing as how your former minder did such a good job watching over you in Pyongyang," the guard continues, "we have invited Comrade Hee-Man to help you adjust to camp life."

It's clear from Hee-Man's body language that he doesn't want to be here any more than I do, and I feel sorry to have dragged my friend into this mess with me.

"You can't keep him here this whole time," I protest weakly. "He has a family to take care of, and he hasn't done anything wrong."

Hee-Man stays silent, and I realize I've spoken out of turn. Thankfully, the guard is quick to assuage my concerns. "This will only be for the first few days. Once you're fully adjusted to camp life, Comrade Hee-Man will be free to leave and return to his adoring family." There's a note of condescension in his voice, and I wonder if there's more to their backstory than I'm aware of. I realize that for all the time Hee-Man and I spent together, I still know very little about his home life.

The guard glances at his watch. "If you'll excuse me, I'm late for an important meeting with the chief officer of productivity." He scowls at Hee-Man as if he were the one to blame for this tardiness. "I'll allow you two to get reacquainted." With that, the guard leaves us alone.

I rush into my apology before Hee-Man can say or do anything else. "I'm so sorry that I'm still causing you all these problems. I hope you know that if it were up to me, you would never have to step foot at a place like this."

Hee-Man shakes his head sadly. "Do not be worried, American. When I heard about your situation, I was happy to volunteer."

I'm surprised by his wording and wonder if Hee-Man truly did have a choice in the matter. But who would request to work at a dismal place like this, even for a few days?

I have no idea how to adequately express my gratitude, and all I can say is, "You look a little fatter than when I saw you last."

He smiles. "And you, American, look thinner." I realize that this is a joke. It won't win us a regular routine on

Saturday Night Live, but it still feels like progress.

Hee-Man passes a cup toward me. "Coffee?"

For a moment, I feel like I'm the luckiest prisoner in all of North Korea. "You must have read my mind."

Giving me a strange glance, probably confused at the idiom, he stands up and brings the coffee over to me before sitting in the chair directly to my left. This is the Hee-Man I remember. Soft-spoken, selfless, and always insisting on invading my personal space.

I love this man. "So what do we do now?" I question. I'm about to ask if he happens to have a flash drive with any other movies. Has he seen *Diehard*? But he sighs heavily, and I know that the moment for joking has passed.

"It is time to start your orientation, American." There's a hint of an unspoken apology in his eyes, and he looks at me. "My job is to help you get settled into camp so you can begin your hard labor sentence right away."

CHAPTER 35

I'm not sure if Hee-Man is always a slowpoke or if he's intentionally taking his time because he knows that as soon as this orientation is over, I begin my hard labor. We've been here alone for two hours already, and I don't know any more about the camp than I did this morning when I woke up alone in my cell.

The North Koreans don't want me mingling with the other prisoners. It makes sense, even though the fact that I'm actually not a spy and have no way to communicate in Korean would make it quite hard for me to spread this dangerous Western propaganda they're so afraid of. But it is what it is, and I can't change any of that. With all the anti-American sentiment in this country, I may be safer on my own anyway.

Hee-Man shows me a few pictures of the men I'll report to. He seems far more familiar than an outside government bureaucrat would be with the inner workings of the camp as he tells me the temperaments of each of my guards.

"So what kind of work are they going to have me do?" I hope he doesn't hear the fear in my voice. For as close as I feel toward Hee-Man right now, I still sense the need to present some kind of a bold front, to ignore the fact that I'm so scared it's a miracle I haven't soiled my prison pants.

Hee-Man takes his time with his answer, and I wonder yet again if he's intentionally stalling on my behalf. "If you were a regular prisoner, you would be sent to the mine, but there is no way you could work down there without coming into contact with the other prisoners."

I suppose this is good news, and I search Hee-Man's expression for signs that he feels the same.

"At a place like this, there are always solitary jobs to be done." He doesn't elaborate, so I'm left with nothing but his cryptic response.

Hee-Man shows me a map of the camp, one of the most helpful parts of this orientation.

"This is where we are." All the writing on the map's in Korean, but I can see that we're toward the west end, just about as far as you can get from the one and only entrance.

"Here is the train station that ships the coal out from the mines," Hee-Man says. "This is the school and the infirmary."

It's like I'm looking at the plans for an entire village. Just how many people live here in this one camp? I remember the group of children I passed only yesterday. How many other minors are here, growing up behind barbed wire, and what sins could they have possibly committed to deserve a fate like this?

"What's over here?" I point toward rows of rectangular buildings on the east side.

"Those are the dorms. That's where most of the other prisoners will stay."

"But not me?"

Hee-Man smiles sadly. "No, not you. I believe the plans for now are to keep you here in underground detainment at night, then let you free during the day."

Free? I wonder if the word means something different to Hee-Man in translation than it does to me. Free would mean I could walk across the street, pull my credit card out of my pocket, and order a triple venti caramel macchiato from Starbucks with a blueberry muffin and a chocolate chip scone on the side.

Free would mean I could buy myself an airplane ticket to Seattle so I could spend the weekend at Grandma Lucy's goat farm.

Oh, well. It's not Hee-Man's fault I am where I am. If anything, it's my fault that he's here, and he's being more than patient with me.

"So what happens to you?" I ask.

"What do you mean?"

"While I'm doing my labor, what will you be doing?"

He nods, his eyes registering his understanding. "I have been assigned to work beside you for the first few days, just until the jailers here are convinced you will not give them any trouble."

"So the harder I work for them, the sooner you can leave camp and go back to your family?"

Hee-Man nods, looking almost embarrassed. "That is correct."

"Then I'll try to do a good job." I force a smile. It's the bold front again, the face I want Hee-Man to see. It's taking nearly all my mental energy to keep from grabbing him and begging him to help me escape.

"Is there any word from Eric Swensson?" I ask instead. "The Swedish guy?"

Hee-Man shakes his head. "Not that I have heard, my friend. I am very sorry. I imagine you are quite homesick."

I don't like the turn this conversation is taking, so I force a smile and clasp him on the back. "Well, hey, I've technically been here a day already. That means I only have seven years, 364 more days to go until I'm out of here, right?"

Hee-Man doesn't respond. I feel the desperate need to make him laugh or chuckle or even smile.

"Right?" I repeat.

He blinks his eyes as if pulling himself out of a trance. "What did you say?"

I repeat the punchline, waiting for his eyes to soften, the corners of his mouth to turn upward in a smile.

"That is a long sentence," Hee-Man says as if to himself. "A long time to stay alive."

CHAPTER 36

It's past midday when Hee-Man steps out to let the guard know I'm ready. My orientation is complete, and my first day of hard labor begins. Since the English-speaking jailor is somewhere else at the moment, I'm depending solely on Hee-Man to serve as my translator.

The guard I report to leads us both outside, and I blink in the harsh light of the sun. Hee-Man thinks it's a good thing I'm being allowed to work in the camp. I guess most of the prisoners in the underground detainment center where I'm to sleep are locked up in solitary confinement for months, maybe even years, at a time.

Logically, I know that hard labor is better than torture, and even torture is better than solitary confinement, at least that's what all the psychological studies on the subject have shown. As far as prisoners at Camp 22 go, I'm one of the lucky ones.

Yes, even here my privilege is starting to show.

The guard leads us toward the barbed wire fence, and

Hee-Man translates my job description. "Do you remember that dried riverbed we passed?"

"Yes."

"He wants you to gather the largest stones from there and bring them here to lay alongside the fence."

"That's it?"

"That is it."

I can think of worse ways to pass an afternoon, not many but at least some. From what Hee-Man already told me, I should be thanking God that I haven't been sent down to the mines like so many of the others here.

Standing on the little hill, I look down the path that will lead me toward the riverbed. "Can you ask him if there's a wheelbarrow or something I can use?"

Hee-Man looks confused.

"Wheelbarrow," I repeat, doing my best impression of a man pushing a cart.

The man hands Hee-Man a burlap sack, and Hee-Man in turn passes it to me. "He says you can use this."

It's not quite what I expected, but at least it's better than the mines. That's going to become my mantra for the afternoon. I can already tell.

I force a grin. "All right." I try to sound as enthusiastic as I can. "Let's go move some rocks."

181

CHAPTER 37

I hate the fact that Hee-Man is here laboring beside me, but when I suggest that he sit back and let me do the heavy lifting, he looks at me as if I've told him one of my favorite American dishes is fried monkey meat.

So we've been working together steadily side by side, and after our first several faltering attempts, we've found a rhythm that's working out well enough. It takes about five minutes to fill the burlap sack half full of stones. That's about as full as we dare. Otherwise we risk ripping the bag, and we'd be stuck shuttling stones up this hill two or three at a time.

Hee-Man carries the bag slung over his shoulder like Santa Claus, and then when we come to the hill I take over. I don't think that's necessarily because I'm stronger than my friend. Right now, if Hee-Man and I were forced to arm wrestle, I'd put my money on him, but when we're by the riverbed, we're fairly secluded. Once we get up the hill, we're in plain view of every single watchtower in this stretch of the perimeter. Since I'm the prisoner, I have to be the one the guards see carrying the stones.

When Hee-Man first explained today's job to me, I had a hard time understanding what the point was. The watchtowers and barbed wire fence are all situated on a hill. Some of the ground beneath the fence is starting to wear away. In a few spots, the erosion has left openings four or five inches deep. There's no real security issue here. Not even a child could fit through a hole that size, and the rocks we set down could just as easily be moved somewhere else, but I suppose the guards have to come up with some way to keep me busy.

The work is physically challenging, especially the last hundred feet or so up this hill, but it's still not as bad as I might have expected. By the time the sun begins to set, I'm blessing Hee-Man for taking so long during my orientation. I know the same job will be waiting for us in the morning, but I'm both relieved and grateful when a bell sounds throughout the camp, and Hee-Man tells me our work is finished.

I'm surprised that no guards come and check our progress, and I wonder if my labor here would be nearly this lenient if Hee-Man weren't with me.

I hate the fact that he's stuck at this place where no sane

human would ever want to venture, but selfishly I'm glad to have him near. I wonder if we're going to sleep in the same room like we did at that hotel in Pyongyang or if the camp administrators have made other arrangements for my friend.

Once we reach the detainment center, Hee-Man stops at a small office inside. He wishes me goodnight, thus answering my question about whether or not we'll remain together, and leaves me with a guard who will take me back downstairs. I don't look back, but I sense Hee-Man's eyes following me until we disappear down the staircase.

It's nice to know that I'll see him tomorrow, and I'm glad for his sake that he doesn't have to spend the night here with me. I hope wherever the camp administrators have put him up he at least has a bed and some source of heat. It's not until I'm locked back in my solitary cell that I realize how exhausted I am from the day's work. My lungs sting, but I don't know if that's because of the recent pneumonia or from carting all those stones uphill all day. The blessing about hard labor is I'm too exhausted to stay up late worrying about my future. I eat the small bowl of soup a guard passes through my door, I lay down on the cold concrete, and within minutes I'm asleep.

CHAPTER 38

Even though I'm in a jail cell in the heart of North Korea, my brain isn't at all surprised to find myself sitting down in Grandma Lucy's dining room for a cup of tea.

She pours the drinks herself and passes me one of her dainty flower teacups.

"So tell me, Ian, what's it like in prison?"

It's as natural as if I were a little boy who just came home from school and she's asking me about my day.

"It's not too bad," I tell her. "I think I'll probably have some blisters on my hands when I wake up, and my back's going to be pretty sore, but other than that, it's all right." I may as well have just told her that my teacher smells like old lady perfume and she doesn't do voices when she reads the books out loud, but otherwise third grade's not half bad.

"Are you making any friends there?" she asks as she serves me up a cinnamon roll that's got to be at least a foot in diameter. I'm going to need some goat milk to wash it down with, and as soon as the thought enters my head, a full glass appears in my hand. Since I know I'm dreaming and that this milk isn't real at all, the materialization makes perfect sense.

"There's one guy who's pretty nice," I answer. "His name's Hee-Man. We get along pretty well."

Grandma Lucy smiles as if I just told her I won the spelling bee in my class. "And is Hee-Man a born-again believer? Does he know Jesus Christ as his personal Lord and Savior?"

It should figure that even in my dream this is the first question Grandma Lucy would ask.

"No, I don't think so."

"Well, why not?"

"Because in North Korea, you get sent to prison if you're a Christian."

"Isn't he already in prison, though?"

"That's different," I tell her, but she's still pushing it.

"If you don't tell him about Jesus, he may never have another chance to receive God's great gift of salvation."

I wish I could be as patient with my grandma in real life as I can in my dream. "I know that's what you think, but I just don't believe the same things anymore."

"Even after God's locked you up in a North Korean prison?"

"Especially after he's locked me up in a North Korean prison."

She stares at me in surprise, as if my conversion post-imprisonment should have been the most natural thing in the world. "You know that if you keep turning your back on him, he's going to keep making it harder for you until you finally acknowledge him as your Lord and Savior."

I want to explain to her how backwards she's making it all sound. Who would want to serve a God who's capricious enough to send his children into torment or suffering just to make them acknowledge him? But I know Grandma Lucy won't see it that way, and I don't want to hurt her feelings. "It's something I'll just have to think about," I say, and seeing as how I have seven years, 364 days of hard labor waiting for me, I don't think I'm going to run out of time very soon.

"Well, I'm going to pray for you right now and ask God to give you a sign."

"You don't have to do that," I tell her, but she insists. Before I know it, her hand is hot against my forehead, and she's praying for me.

"Father God, Maker of the universe, King and Sovereign over all creation, we proclaim you as Lord. We proclaim you as King in North Korea as you are in heaven. We proclaim that your plans for my grandson are for good and that he is not forgotten or abandoned. We proclaim blessings and health over him. May you strengthen him to carry on the work he's been called to do, and may you keep his spirit and soul from despair. I pray that when he wakes up, everlasting joy will crown his head, that hope will swell deep in his spirit, that your courage will flow through his veins.

"I pray your comfort over him, Lord. Comfort my grandson and let him know that you love him more than he'll ever understand. Teach him that you are good and that your plans for him are good. Show him how much you love him. Send him hope. Send him a reminder of your love so that the very moment he wakes up, he'll be unable to deny that you are with him, that you are his God and that you are worthy of all his worship and all his devotion. We pray this in the beloved, powerful, and precious name of Jesus Christ, who came down from heaven to redeem us sinners from our sins. Amen."

She takes her hand off my forehead and looks at me. "How was that?"

"Really nice," I answer, "but I don't think I'm going to feel different when I wake up."

She gives me a sly smile, and even as she's fading out of sight, I'm pretty sure I can see her wink.

"You'll see," she says as she disappears from view. "You'll see."

The morning alarm goes off and the electric light overhead zaps on. I lay still for a moment in silent introspection, trying to figure out if anything has changed. My forehead itches where she touched it, but other than that, I'm just as hungry, just as cold, and just as tired as I was when I went to bed. I let out my breath.

Thanks for trying, Grandma Lucy, I say to the phantom from my dream. *Maybe next time.*

CHAPTER 39

"Are you superstitious?" I ask Hee-Man that afternoon as we fill up our sack with rocks.

"Am I what?"

"Superstitious. Like when you think seeing a black cat will bring you bad luck, or you toss salt over your shoulder if you accidentally break a mirror."

He stares at me like I've grown a second nose without realizing it. "Why would I do that?"

"Never mind." I'm still thinking about what happened last night. From a psychological standpoint, it makes perfect sense why my brain would conjure up an image of Grandma Lucy and let me talk to her in my dream, especially since I've missed her so much.

"What about dreams?" I ask Hee-Man as he hefts the bag over his shoulder with a groan.

We start the trek out of the woods and toward the hill.

"What about them?"

"Do you think they ever mean anything special?"

190

"Of course they do."

Now we're onto something. "Like what?"

"What do you mean? Did you have a dream last night?"

For some reason, I'm reluctant to tell him what happened. This meeting with Grandma Lucy, even though it was entirely made up in my brain, feels private. Something that was just for me. But I tell him the basics anyway. "Not many people in the States would think it means anything other than the fact that I'm homesick."

Hee-Man shakes his head as if he feels sorry for all of us stupid, brainwashed Americans.

We're out of the woods. It's my turn to take the sack now and carry it the rest of the way up the hill. "Do you think it means anything?" I ask.

"Certainly." I don't have to give him any more of an invitation to interpret the dream for me. "The food you were eating, that means that soon you will receive a large meal. Sitting down with your grandmother, that means your meal is going to be with someone very important. Someone with a lot of authority. You say your grandmother prayed for you, is that right? That she asked for your release?"

"Yes," I answer, but now as I say the words I can't remember if Grandma Lucy prayed for my release or just offered up the same flowery phrases as usual.

Hee-Man smiles. "That's easy. It means that soon someone very important is going to come and eat a big meal with you, and they will report your case to your president to ask him to beg Pyongyang for your release."

I have no idea why he sounds so certain or how my Grandma's praying for me could somehow foretell a meeting with some important advocate, but he seems so convinced I decide to put it to the test.

All right, God, I pray. *Grandma Lucy mentioned asking you for a sign, so here's what it is. If you're really out there looking out for me like she says, then I want you to make everything Hee-Man just told me come true.*

I glance over at my friend and think I detect a slight smirk on his face. Was this his version of a joke? Is he mocking me after I shared something as personal as the dream I had last night about my grandma? I don't care. I've already prayed my prayer, and if God wants to do anything about it, he knows where to find me.

One more thing, I add to my bargain with the Almighty. *That meal Hee-Man mentioned? I want it to be steak. A big, juicy beefsteak. Otherwise, we have no deal.*

Now it's my turn to smirk because I know that in this land of famine and hunger and scarcity, there's absolutely no way anybody, no matter how important, is going to manage to get a steak dinner into the prison camp to share with one of North Korea's allegedly dangerous criminals.

I carry the bag of rocks the rest of the way up the hill, feeling thankful that I'm not the type of person to fall prey to foolish superstitions or blind faith. That sort of thinking does nothing but set you up for disappointment. I'm not going to stop hoping for my release, but I know that when and if that day comes, it's going to be because I was resourceful. I was strong. I was the one who refused to give in to despair.

I'm the only one looking out for me right now. I'm my own biggest advocate. And if I can just keep my mind clear, if I can keep putting one foot in front of the other and keep on finishing the work these men give me to do, I'm going to be just fine.

CHAPTER 40

"*Yesunim-ui guwon.*"

I open my eyes at the strange sound. Someone is talking in one of the other cells. It's a woman, and judging by the cracks in her voice, she's just as old as my Grandma Lucy or even older.

"*Yesunim-ui guwon.*" She's repeating the same phrases over and over, each time with even more passion and intensity in her tone. I've never heard the words before, but there's something familiar about the way she speaks them.

I have no idea what time it is, but since I'm not horrifically tired and the electricity still hasn't been turned on I guess it's early morning, just before sunrise.

I try to think through last night, but my brain is foggy. Hee-Man and I spent the day working together and parted ways when the evening bell rang. Then what? I came here. My talk with Hee-Man got me thinking about a steak dinner. That's probably why my sleep was so fitful. Even though I knew his prediction about my dream was about as likely as

194

ALANA TERRY

NASA sending a bunch of roughneck oil drillers into space to detonate an asteroid, Hee-Man actually had me going. Actually had me wondering if someone was about to waltz into my room, tell me I had an important guest visiting, and offer me a steak.

I'm no prophet, but I'm pretty certain that my next steak meal won't be for another seven years and 363 days.

I'm straining my ears, trying to figure out if I heard an actual noise that woke me up or if it was just part of my dream. But then I hear it again.

"Yesunim-ui guwon."

I'll have to try to remember the phrase so I can ask Hee-Man what it means. The speaker is repeating the words with an energy and passion that reminds me of Grandma Lucy praying.

"Yesunim-ui guwon."

I hate the fact that as soon as she stops saying these words, I'm going to forget them. I can't keep anything straight in my mind right now. I don't know if that's because I'm always hungry or always tired or always working. All I know is I no longer possess the mental acuity that allowed me to earn my undergrad and graduate degrees from a school like Harvard.

"Yesunim-ui guwon."

195

I want to call out to her, ask her what she's saying, but I'm certain it wouldn't do anything other than scare her into shutting up. Nobody down here speaks English. And I have to admit that hearing her voice, any voice at all actually, reminds me that I'm not alone. The more I listen, the more I wonder if she really is praying. The only other time I've ever heard someone sound so passionate is when Grandma Lucy talks to the Lord. Sometimes she gets into a fit like this too, saying the same thing over and over and over.

"Yesunim-ui guwon." The words take on an almost desperate tone. I don't like to admit that I'm frightened, but I want to know what this old woman's saying. Is she trying to communicate with me? Is she calling down curses on us? For all I know, she's about to have a heart attack, and she's begging the guards for help.

If I had a pillow, I'd cover my ears. If I had music, I'd blast it at full volume to drown out her voice, but here all I can do is listen.

"Yesunim-ui guwon."

I whisper the words to myself, trying to guess what they might mean, begging my brain to remember so I can ask Hee-Man later when we're working.

Eventually her voice dies down, and I realize how tired I still am. I assume the lights will probably turn on any minute, and I'll be faced with yet another day of hard labor. Hee-Man hasn't said so directly, but I've got the feeling this is going to be his last day with me as well, so you can imagine I'm not looking forward to morning.

I lean against the wall. I don't even bother trying to lie down, and I will myself to drift back off into sleep. The old woman down here has stopped her prayers or crying or chants or whatever it is she's been doing, but I can still hear the echoes of her words in my mind. I say them to myself over and over, like a lullaby.

Yesunim-ui guwon.

CHAPTER 41

"Easy," Hee-Man tells me that morning when I ask him to translate the old woman's words. "She must be one of those Christians like you have in America."

"Why do you say that?" I ask, and for a moment I worry if I'm going to get my friend in trouble by bringing this up at all.

"She is saying *Jesus saves*, that is all."

"Oh." I wait. For as enchanted and haunting as that old woman's words sounded in my cell, I was expecting to feel something different when I figured out what they meant. Turns out the speaker's nothing but a religious fanatic like my grandma. I wonder how long she's been in underground detainment.

Hee-Man and I focus on filling the burlap sack, but as he makes his way through the trail leading out of the woods, I decide to ask him something.

"I've noticed you seem to know a lot about camp life here." I gauge his reaction out of the corner of my eye.

198

"Yes."

"I was just wondering if you've worked with anyone like me before. Anything like that."

He sighs. I'm pretty sure I said something wrong, and he'll spend the next half hour refusing to answer any question directly. He confirmed this morning that he'll be leaving after our shift is over, and I really don't want to end things on an awkward note.

"It's probably none of my business," I add. "It just got me curious."

Hee-Man hands me the sack. It's a little sooner than where we normally trade off, but seeing as how after today I'll be forced to do this job entirely on my own, I'm not going to complain if he shorts me a few dozen yards.

"Do you know who Choi Jun-Ho is?" he asks.

I shake my head.

"Maybe you know him by his American name. Brad Thomas."

"Oh, right." I should have remembered. The Korean-American pastor was all over the news a few years ago when he was arrested in North Korea after leading a prayer group to Pyongyang.

Hee-Man glances over at me, and I can't tell if he looks proud or embarrassed. "I was assigned to his case."

"Oh." I wasn't expecting that. For starters, it seems like the kind of thing Hee-Man would have mentioned much earlier in our relationship. *Hey, want to know something interesting? You're not the first American prisoner I've taken care of.*

"Why didn't you tell me this sooner?" It could have done wonders to break the ice early on.

Hee-Man can't meet my gaze. "You never asked."

I decide to let it drop, at least that part of it. "So is this the same prison camp he was sent to?" I've listened to the one and only press interview Pastor Brad gave after his release, but he made it very clear he didn't want to divulge any details or speak about what happened to him when he was in North Korea.

Hee-Man nods. "Yes. This is how I know the schedule and the guards."

I try to remember more about Pastor Brad's case. He was held here longer than any other American since the Korean War. "How long was he at camp?" I'm not sure I want to know. Not sure his is a record I'd like to break.

"Fourteen months."

I don't say anything. First of all, we're at the hill now, and I have to focus all my energy on just getting these rocks up to the top. You'd think the work would get easier after the first few days, but all that's happening is I'm getting more exhausted, more easily winded, and more blistered.

"How did Pastor Brad get out of here?" I've heard the American news reports on the subject of course, but I also know there must have been plenty going on behind the scenes that was never disclosed.

"He was given a medical release when he fell extremely ill." Hee-Man doesn't offer any more information, and I sense it's not my place to pry. Or maybe I just don't want to know. Don't want to face that my stay here at Camp 22 could stretch out for as long as his ... or even longer.

We're all the way back at the stream when Hee-Man says quietly, "He wanted me to convert."

I don't know if it's the way he's whispering or the danger inherent in a word like *convert* in a place like this, but I feel my pulse surging in my ears. "What do you mean?

"We spent a lot of time together, and he wanted me to become a Christian and believe like he did."

The most natural question in the world would be to ask Hee-Man if he did convert, if he turned to this American's God and asked Jesus to forgive his sins. But something keeps me from opening my mouth. I've been in here long enough to know that the last thing I want to do is force my friend to say something that could get him in so much trouble.

We say nothing until our sack is full and we're halfway out of the woods. "He was a good man," Hee-Man announces. "Sometimes I miss him."

I wonder if years from now, when I'm safe at home and fattening myself up on Aunt Connie's cinnamon rolls, Hee-Man will look back and say the same thing about me.

CHAPTER 42

The power hasn't gone out for the night, but I'm already locked in my underground detainment cell when I hear voices outside. There's a rattle at my door, and I stand up to meet whoever has come to see me.

It's Hee-Man.

"What are you doing here? I thought you went home already."

"Soon." He smiles softly. "I came to give something to my American friend. A parting gift."

Hee-Man has done a fabulous job popping in and out of my life at just the right time. I don't like the finality I hear in his words.

I stare at the book in his hands. "My grandma's Bible?"

"I asked the chief officer to make a special exception so you could have this. I think it's what your grandmother would have wanted."

I don't know what to say. Just the sight of the worn leather binding is enough to melt me into a puddle of emotions. "Thank you."

Hee-Man extends his hand for a formal American handshake. I wonder if he notices the way my lip is trembling.

"Will you come to see me sometimes?" I ask faintly. "Is that kind of thing allowed?"

Hee-Man's smile is soft and paternal. "I would like that, American. But what I would like even more is to know that you are safe at home among your own people."

"You and me both," I mutter.

"I do not believe that time is too far off. Remember your dream."

I can't believe he's still harping on that silly interpretation he gave me about those cinnamon rolls and Grandma Lucy's prayers. I smile, grateful that at least we'll get to end this meeting on a happy note. "I don't think I'll be having a steak dinner any time soon."

He's staring at me quizzically, like he knows a secret I don't. "We will see, American. We will see."

I want to hug him, but I'm embarrassed to admit I don't even know how to initiate that sort of a farewell. All the people I hug are little old ladies like my Aunt Connie who just jump right in and wrap their arms around my neck whether I want them to or not. Instead, I extend my hand once more. I wonder when the next time I'll come into physical contact with a human being will be, at least a human being whose job isn't to beat or torture me.

"Take care of yourself, American. And greet your grandmother when you see her."

He turns away, but not before I detect a quiver in his chin. Then the door shuts and I'm left alone again in the darkness.

CHAPTER 43

The next morning a sour-faced guard appears at the entrance of my cell. His voice is high-pitched and impatient. I can't understand what he's saying but assume he's ordering me out to work. I was expecting something like this. Now that Hee-Man's back home with his family, my labor will be monitored by one of the random guards assigned to the underground detainment center.

We step outside, and I see the guard's blinking just as much as I am in the early morning light. Since nobody's told me otherwise, I assume I'm meant to return to the spot where I gathered rocks to place in front of the barbed-wire fence. Somehow I doubt my new caretaker is going to get his hands dirty helping me like Hee-Man did.

It's cold, probably the coldest morning since I arrived at Camp 22. When we get near the riverbed, I glance over at my new babysitter. He gives a grunt, the universal sign for *Get to work*. He rubs his hands together, and I can see his breath. He can't be any more comfortable than I am, but at least I get to move around. The young man seems to be content with watching me from a distance. I'm ready for someone to talk to. I'm not even half an hour into my workday, and already I miss Hee-Man with an emptiness that's almost tangible.

With the work we've already done, there's very few rocks large enough left at this part of the riverbed. I head farther downstream, my chaperone remaining ten or twenty yards away.

"Wish you were here instead of this guy," I mumble. I'm not talking to myself, which would make me question my sanity. I'm talking to Hee-Man even though he's miles away. "So the steak dinner you promised me still hasn't come. What have you got to say about that?"

Talking to an invisible Hee-Man passes the time almost as well as it did when he was still here. The convenient part is I don't have to wait for his response.

"You're smart to have left when you did. Smart to be as far away as you can get before winter hits."

I'm trying not to focus on the dropping temperatures, but if my guards expect me to do manual labor outdoors for twelve hours a day in nothing but my prison uniform, I'll be an icicle by Christmas.

"You'd enjoy Christmas in America." I tell Hee-Man all

about our traditions, carols, and the candlelight service at Grandma Lucy's small country church. "One year you can fly out to Washington, you and your family, and we'll all celebrate Christmas together." I feel a small surge of hope until I realize that I'm talking to a phantom friend about a dream that could never come true.

I'm halfway up the hill with my bundle of rocks when I pass three children. I can't tell how old they are. To my American eye they look small enough to be in kindergarten, but I'm guessing they must be older than that to be allowed out here alone. I glance at my guard, who makes no move to run them off or report their truancy to any authorities.

They're wearing what I assume is an approximation of school uniforms, but even in this cold they're barefoot. That's not what's most striking, though. What's most striking is the way they're staring at me with the exact same look of mistrust and disgust I see in the eyes of my guards.

These children hate me.

I make a growl and scare them off with a sudden stomp of my foot, and they take off scampering. The guard laughs, but I don't bother to look at him. Instead I focus on this hill I'm supposed to climb with this sack of rocks on my back. I'll probably make twenty more trips here before the workday's over, and already I feel like I need a nap.

"See what happens when you're not here to keep me in line?" I ask Hee-Man. "I go around scaring poor children for laughs."

In my mind, I see my friend's face smiling at me sadly.

My stomach grumbles.

I'm still waiting for that steak dinner.

CHAPTER 44

It's late in the afternoon, but judging by the position of the sun, I've still got over an hour's worth of work left before the evening bell rings. A week or longer has passed since Hee-Man took off. I'm still shuffling rocks up this hill, still talking to my imaginary friend. The only difference is the temperature has continued to drop. This morning, the entire camp was covered with frost.

It's times like this I'm thankful for the physical activity. Just a few trips up and down that hill and I start to sweat.

"You know," I say to my invisible friend, "this was easier when you were actually here to help."

I'm not mad at Hee-Man for abandoning me. If I had a family to go home to and permission to leave, I wouldn't have even stuck around for that last goodbye, but I find myself praying more and more that I'll get to see Hee-Man again before my release.

I've already come to the conclusion that my eight-year sentence was just for show. It was to force the US government into action. Now Washington has to apologize for me, do a little bit of diplomatic groveling, and then North Korea can send me away. I'm not doing anything productive for them while I'm here. These rocks I'm moving day in and day out are no better by the fence than the riverbed. It can't be an efficient use of resources to keep me under the watchful eye of a guard every hour of the day either.

North Korea wants to get rid of me almost as badly as I want to be rid of them.

It's just a matter of my government playing this little political game the right way. Then I'm going home. Because I may have started the summer as a strong, healthy young man, but I know for a fact I won't last here a full eight years.

I've always been one to watch what I say. I'm all for positive thinking, self-motivation, the works. I'm careful with my words, even my thoughts. Instead of saying *My photography's never going to get me anywhere*, I'd say *I wonder what it will feel like the day I learn I've been nominated for a Pulitzer prize.* I'm certain these pep talks are one of the reasons my career has carried me as far as it has.

But there's keeping a positive slant on things, and there's lying to yourself. I'm not stupid enough that I can force myself to believe outright deceit. Sometimes you've just got to face up to facts. I can't survive eight years of this. I'm already mentally and physically at the bottom of a very long rope. My optimism and humor have carried me this far, but now I'm at the end of this string where I find myself dangling above a very precarious chasm.

So instead of focusing on eight years, I talk to Hee-Man about my release.

"I wonder who they'll send to pick me up. The Vice President, perhaps? Although I wonder if this is more of a job for the Secretary of State. When that American pastor got arrested, it was one of the former presidents who came to collect him. I wonder what that would be like. Would I end up with my own secret service detail, do you think?"

Hee-Man remains silent as always, but that doesn't slow down my monologue.

"You know, that was a pretty mean trick you pulled with your whole dream interpretation thing. Look at me. Still no steak dinner, but now I'm fixating on it, thanks to you."

Sometimes when I'm especially hungry and I know my guard is well out of earshot, I tell Hee-Man about all the food I'm sure my Aunt Connie would cook up for us if we ever took a pitstop to Orchard Grove. "You ever had goat's milk? It's not quite as creamy as cow's, but it's sweeter. Once you get used to it, there's no going back. Do you know what shepherd's pie is? I think it's originally an English dish. Maybe Scottish. You take all kinds of vegetables and meat, slather on a bunch of gravy, and top it with mashed potatoes, cheese, and a whole lot of paprika. You're lucky because there's nobody in the US who makes shepherd's pie as well as my aunt, and I'm sure that's what she's going to cook up for us. I hope you like dessert too. Ever had a cinnamon roll?"

In the back of my mind, I'm not sure if I should consider myself ingenious for finding this way to pass the time or if I should worry about my sanity. I don't bother to ask Hee-Man his opinion on the subject. It's one of the only things we don't talk about.

"I sure wish you'd tell me if you were a Christian, Hee-Man. I think it'd explain an awful lot about you if I knew you were a secret believer." Of course, I have to be very careful even talking to my imaginary friend about things like this, and I usually only do it when I know my guard's far enough away and looking especially distracted.

"I guess you could say I was pretty religious growing up. Kind of like all of you in North Korea, in a parallel way at least. You don't know anything other than your little socialist dictatorship. I didn't know anything other than conservative Christianity. I didn't feel like it was oppressive. It wasn't until I moved out that I discovered the universe was a lot bigger than I'd been taught."

I sigh. The Hee-Man in my brain isn't quite as good of a conversational partner as the one in real life.

"But I've been reading my grandma's Bible sometimes," I tell him when I'm feeling especially talkative. "It was nice of you to bring that to me." I don't like to admit to Hee-Man how lonely I get at night in that underground detention center, but I think it's one of those things he knows without being told.

"My grandma wrote a lot of notes in the page margins," I say. "I've spent more time reading the prayers she's written out than the actual verses." I wonder what Grandma Lucy would think of this confession. Would she be hopeful that somehow her faith expressed in her prayers will rub off on me? Or would she be disappointed that I'm reading her words instead of the ones of her beloved Savior?

"Ever heard the story of Elijah?" I ask the silence. "He was hungry once when he was hiding from a deranged queen, so God sent ravens to bring him crumbs of food each day." I give a little chuckle. "It's a good thing he wasn't so hungry he ate the ravens instead, right?"

There's an awkward silence, and I clear my throat. "Hee-man? Can I tell you something?"

I pause to wait for the answer that's only in my mind.

"I'm getting more and more afraid. Winter's coming soon, and I really don't know how I'm going to survive it when it hits."

CHAPTER 45

When I step outside one morning and see a thin blanket of snow covering the prison campgrounds, my heart sinks as quickly as my teeth start to chatter. I don't think it's particularly colder than it's been over the past few days, but something about seeing the snow on the ground makes it feel that much worse.

We're deep into November now. I know because I've been counting down the days until my birthday.

Which is today. Happy birthday to me.

I wonder if this layer of snow is God's sick and twisted practical joke. I hope he knows me well enough to understand I wouldn't find this funny at all.

It's been weeks since I finished up the job by the riverbank. Lately, I've been spending my days stacking crates of coal behind a large train depot, but this morning as I head out to my usual spot, the guard assigned to me shouts something and stands in my way. I have no idea what he says, but I know I'm supposed to follow.

216

At least there'll be something new today. As an environmentalist, I'm not sure how I feel about stacking those crates of coal anyway.

The guard leads me across the camp. I've never been in this part of the compound before. I pass the school where I hear children chanting out their lessons, then we make our way to the dorms, currently abandoned while all the adults are at their work details.

The guard points to two handleless buckets. I pick them up automatically and follow him behind the dorms. Even in this cold, my nose tells me what's coming before I see the rows of outhouses.

At least I'm not in the coal mines, I remind myself, and after an accident last week injured what I can only guess was scores of workers down there, it's not that hard to feel grateful.

Even as I'm forced to scoop out the human waste beneath the outhouses and carry them to a plot of ground near the mess hall. I assume that in the spring my labor will fertilize the soil where the camp's food will grow, and I try to find yet another reason to give thanks.

Better soil means more food, which means I might not be so close to starving when spring comes.

It's the thought that fuels my aching muscles, the

promise that strengthens my exhausted body. The rattle in my lungs is back again. I noticed it nearly a week ago but had nobody to tell except for Hee-Man, who I'm starting to worry was never more than this phantom in my head. Maybe there never was a Hee-Man. Maybe watching *Armageddon* together in Pyongyang was a hallucination.

I've given up any hope for a steak dinner. Right now, I'd settle for a bowl of rice. The few kernels of corn I get mashed up into some sort of saltless, tasteless gruel isn't enough to support the twelve hours of work I do every day. When I sink down against my cement wall at night, I can't rest my forehead against my knees because they've grown too jagged.

At least I'm not getting tortured. I can hear the tormented cries of prisoners on the level above me when I head upstairs to work every day, and I remind myself that I have dozens, probably hundreds of reasons to give thanks. It's all I have to focus on while I fertilize this field with human waste.

I'm close enough to the school that I can hear the chants of the children when I empty the contents of my slop buckets on the frozen ground. I wish Hee-Man were here to tell me what they're saying. I'm so distracted I must have been neglecting my work because the guard snaps something at me and I realize I've been staring at the children through a window.

Unfortunately, the guard's yelling is enough to attract the attention of the teacher. She storms out and grabs me by the ear as if I were one of her unruly students. I'm too tired to be surprised, too drained to wonder what's supposed to happen next. She drags me inside and marches me to the front of the class as if I were the pet and she were the student delivering her show-and-tell. I wonder if there'll be a question and answer session next. *What does he eat? How do you bathe him? Does he bite? Can I pet him?*

For a moment, I think she's lecturing me, but I realize she's yelling at her pupils. At first, people who saw me in the camp looked afraid, but that must have been when I still looked like someone who could hurt them if I tried. I still remember with shame the day I growled at the kids who only stopped for a moment to stare. I wonder if any of them are in this class, but I'm so used to my position as a prisoner, as a subordinate, that I don't even raise my eyes to scan their faces.

Then all of a sudden the teacher is yelling at me, and I step back like a mangy dog afraid of getting kicked. The students laugh, and the teacher encourages them with her taunts. I have no idea what she's saying. *Look at the ugly*

American. See his big nose? She might be telling them I'm a bogeyman who'll sneak into their dorms and try to eat their toes if they're not careful. All I know is whatever she's saying is making her class laugh and point, and tears of humiliation streak down my cheeks, which only seems to fuel their mass cruelty.

My guard appears at the door and snaps something at the teacher. He yells something at me next, which I take to mean my humiliation is over. It's time to return to digging out waste from underneath the outhouses.

I focus again on all that I have to be thankful for.

At least I'm not being tortured. At least I'm not one of the workers injured in the mines. At least I don't have to stand in front of that class anymore.

Cold tears still leak down my face, and I'm grateful my guard doesn't seem to notice or care. I pick up my two buckets, thankful for mindless work, looking forward expectantly to spring when the fruits of my labor will mean a garden fit to feed us prisoners.

I'm crying as I go about my labor, and the tears splash silently onto the snowy mush beneath my feet.

CHAPTER 46

There's an angry commotion when my guard returns me to the underground detainment center that night. I don't know what the fighting's about, nor do I question it. In just a moment I'll be walked downstairs and locked in my cage, and ten or fifteen minutes after that, someone will pass a tasteless dinner into my cell.

That's all I care about at the moment. My two hundred calories.

I cough weakly. If Hee-Man were here, I think he'd be worried about the sound I make when I breathe, but nobody seems to notice.

The guards argue more than normal, and my only hope is that I have the strength and energy to stand here until they resolve whatever issues they're having with one another. Don't they know I just want to go to my cell?

"Prisoner 249." It's an English-speaking guard, perhaps the one I met my first day here. I'm too tired to wonder what he wants with me. Dinner is in only ten minutes. I can't afford to be late.

He joins the snappy fight. I want to find a way to tell him I'm not worth arguing over. *Just take me to my cell and give me my corn. That's all I ask. I've earned it.*

He turns his nose up at me. "Is there somewhere you can wash?" he demands.

I shrug. Shouldn't he know that better than I?

Finally, he says something that sends one of his inferiors scurrying. They come back in a minute with a bucket and a brush, the kind you'd use to scrub the floor. Don't they realize the evening bell already rang? I did my work today. It's time for my meal.

Sharp fingers pinch me. My bicep is so small the man can wrap his hand around my arm. I wince, not from the pain but from the realization that I may miss my dinner tonight. He can check the records himself. I worked my full shift. It's time for my food.

I'm in a small room, no bigger than a closet. I'm stripped down, and two men start splashing cold water over my body, scrubbing me with a brush that carries its own very suspicious smell and stains. I'm thankful for my bath, but I'm begging God that it won't mean I have to miss my meal.

They argue some more before someone comes in and tosses over a set of prison clothes. They're the same style as what I normally wear, except not so threadbare. "Look at me," I want to tell Hee-Man. "It's *Extreme Makeover: Prison Camp Edition*." I know then I'd have to explain my joke, which by definition would mean it would no longer be funny, but I chuckle to myself anyway.

They can keep me alive by feeding me three or four hundred calories a day. They can parade me in front of their classrooms to mock me and taunt me and put me on display like an animal in a zoo. They can order me to carry buckets of waste for twelve hours a day in the snow.

But they can't take away my sense of humor.

Hear that, guards? You can't have it. You wouldn't know what to do with it even if you did.

I can't say why, but the thought makes me chuckle again. I think they're mad at me, but what do I care? It's almost my dinner time. Nothing's getting between me and my few bites of gruel.

They lead me out of the showering room. It's like I'm an entirely new prisoner. I wonder what it all means, and what does it matter as long as they lock me up downstairs in time to get fed?

"Ian?"

I blink. I know that face. Where have I seen him before? He reaches out his hand. "Do you know who I am?"

"Mr. Swede," I respond with a chuckle.

"Swensson," he corrects. "Eric Swensson."

"Eric Swensson the Swede." I laugh at my joke and wonder why he doesn't join in.

"Would you care for dinner?" he asks.

I look at his small pot belly, his trimmed goatee, his clean shoes. "Only if it's steak," I answer, but the laugh I expect never comes.

The Swedish ambassador looks stern. I feel like I should apologize. *I tried to change into nicer clothes, but this was all I could find on such short notice.*

Why isn't he laughing? Doesn't he realize how hilarious I am?

"What's wrong with him?" he barks.

"Nothing," the guard assures him. "Nothing. He just likes to keep us all amused."

Eric frowns at me, and again I feel like I should apologize. But for what?

A minute later, we're in a conference room, just him and me. I think it's the same room where I met with Hee-Man my first full day here, but now I can't be entirely sure that Hee-Man ever even existed, let alone met with me in this exact location.

"Have a seat, Ian."

For a moment, I'm certain that I've been given the miraculous ability to understand Korean. Then I remember he speaks English.

I sink into my chair. "It's dinnertime," I feel compelled to remind him.

I wish he wouldn't look at me like that. I don't know what I did to make him so upset, but if he could just tell me, I could go ahead and apologize and get this awkward meeting over with. If they don't find me in my cell when they're passing out the food, what if they skip my room altogether?

"I ordered you some dinner," he tells me. "We'll eat together in just a few minutes."

I want to ask him if he likes corn gruel, but I can't get over the fact that he looks so angry at me. I'm afraid.

He sighs and leans forward. "What have they been doing to you, Ian? Are they treating you poorly?"

I shake my head.

"Are they withholding your food rations?"

I have to think about this for a moment. I've always assumed that the food is reduced here because it's winter now and calories are harder to come by all around. I'm never with anyone else when I eat, so I have no way to know if I'm being cheated out of my fair share or not. The thought makes my heart ache. What if someone's taking some of my dinner each night?

Eric sighs. "I came here to tell you that your government hasn't forgotten about your case. Things are still moving, even if it seems like all is silent."

His words rush in and out of focus in my ears. I'm trying to decide if this really was the room where I met with Hee-Man, if Hee-Man truly exists, and if this Swedish ambassador did or didn't say I'd be back in my cell in time for dinner. Why can't I keep any of it straight in my head?

There's a knock at the door. Eric smiles for the first time since he's seen me.

He sets a plate before me. "I heard a rumor that it's a special day today. Happy birthday, Ian, from all of us at the Swedish embassy and all your friends and family back home."

Silent sobs wrack my body. I wish Hee-Man were here to see this. He's the only one who would understand. He could tell the Swede why I'm crying.

On the plate in front of me is a sizzling steak dinner.

CHAPTER 47

It's amazing how quickly a little bit of protein revives me. Eric urges me to eat slowly, but I suspect he's never existed for months on nothing but corn gruel.

The Swedish ambassador holds out a small voice recorder, and he's asking me questions about my detainment. "Have you been mistreated?" he asks, and I shake my head. I know he can't record that on the gadget of his, but my mouth is too full to answer properly.

"Are you warm enough at night?"

That one's even easier. "No."

"Are you forced to work?"

"Yes."

"What do they make you do?"

"Move things." I answer as succinctly as I can to give my mouth the time it needs to chew. I want to find whoever cooked this steak and hire him to become my personal chef for the rest of my entire life.

"What kinds of things?" Eric asks.

"Buckets."

He stares at me. I realize I'm probably not being the model witness he wants me to be, but what does he expect? I have steak.

"How is your health?" he asks. "Are you ill?"

I shrug. "Probably."

"Could you be more specific, Ian? Could you tell me some of your symptoms?" He's being patient with me, like a father teaching his kid to ride his bike for the first time.

"I'm hungry." Is that a symptom? All of a sudden I'm not sure.

"Anything else?" Eric holds out his device, ready to capture my response.

"A cough."

He nods. "I want a doctor to check you out."

I swallow a bite of steak and go for another. I'm sure I'll be embarrassed to look back and remember tonight. Eric had to cut the meat for me. My hands were shaking so much I couldn't handle the knife, and I think he was afraid if he didn't do something, I'd put the entire slab into my mouth at once. It took him several minutes, but he ended up giving me bites hardly larger than peas. I want to find out his address. I bet Grandma Lucy will want to send him a Christmas card and ask him if he's been born again.

When I'm halfway through dinner, Eric steps outside to use his phone. I can hear him talking in the hallway, clearly agitated. Either he's speaking Swedish or I've momentarily lost my ability to decipher English, but either way I don't care.

Because steak.

"All right, Ian," he tells me when he comes back in. I stare at him like a dog caught with its nose in the trashcan. I wasn't supposed to put so much food in my mouth at once, but I didn't realize he'd get off the phone so soon. "We're going to get you to the hospital. I want them to give you a full exam."

Right now? What about my dinner?

He stands over me and rubs my back when I start to cough out my precious hoard of meat. "Don't worry," he says, "we're going to get you the care you need."

CHAPTER 48

I'm back at the Pyongyang hospital. Doc seems happy to see me but just as quickly turns sad again when he presses his cold stethoscope up against my chest. I'm too busy staring out the window to pay him much attention.

Where's my dog? What happened to Rusty? I keep waiting for his paws to press up against the glass, for his nose to press into the pane and fog up the entire thing.

Where did my dog go? Why isn't he here to say hello?

After Doc examines me, the Swede pulls up a chair. I feel like a little kid whose father is about to read him a bedtime story.

"Ian, you're very ill," Eric says. "It's quite serious."

I nod. I think I could have told him that and saved everyone a lot of time.

"I'm going to make sure you don't have to go back to that prison camp."

"Okay," I tell him, but what I really want to know is if he's seen a mangy, ugly mutt running around the courtyard.

"The doctor wants to give you antibiotics. They're also going to put some nutrients in your IV. You're extremely malnourished."

Yes, I think that's what tends to happen when you're forced to do hard labor on nothing but a few hundred calories of corn paste a day, but I don't say anything.

"I'm going to check on you in the morning, but first I want you to have something." Eric reaches into his back pocket and pulls out an envelope. "This is from your Grandma Lucy. We have several hundred other letters waiting for you at our embassy, but this is all I was allowed to bring for the moment."

"Is it a birthday card?" I ask.

Eric's eyes are full of sadness. No matter what I say, I can't seem to get the man to smile. It's like he doesn't even know when I'm joking or not.

He places his hand on my shoulder then winces. I want to apologize for being so bony that I hurt him, but even more than that I want to find something funny to say to lift the mood if only for a moment.

"Take care of yourself," he says softly, "and don't worry. You're in good hands now." At least I think that's what he says, but as he leaves I realize he might have told me I'm in God's hands. Now that he's gone, there's really no way to be sure which it was.

I look at the envelope he gave me. A letter from my Grandma Lucy. I should have figured she'd never forget my birthday.

I open it up.

I'm starving for some news from home.

CHAPTER 49

Dear Ian,

It's getting close to Thanksgiving now, and I pray this letter will reach you in time for me to wish you a very blessed holiday. And a happy birthday too. You know it's my tradition to call you on your birthday and pray for you. Of course, that's a little difficult right now, so I'm going to write out my prayer and trust God that it reaches you at just the right time.

I take in each word, pausing because my eyes are unaccustomed to my grandma's small, slanted handwriting.

You are a beloved child of the King. I still remember the day you made your profession of faith at Vacation Bible School. You remember that? And I know since then you've wandered away from the truth, but I'm clinging to God's promises that no sheep is ever snatched out of the hands of the Good Shepherd.

Something stirs in my spirit, a memory. Walking down the aisle, telling the VBS worker I want to be saved. Letting

Grandma Lucy know I accepted Jesus into my heart. The excitement that followed as Aunt Connie made me an enormous cake to celebrate my salvation experience.

You are his child, Ian, whether you acknowledge him as your Father or not. And whatever trials you've been forced to endure, he's been there beside you. He's the strength that whispers hope to your weary soul when you feel you can't go on. He's the courage that wells up inside you when you're confronted with unspeakable evil. He's the friend who whispers peace to you when the darkness tempts you toward despair. He is your rescuer, your shield, and your refuge, and no matter how far you may think you've wandered away from him, he's been right there beside you all this time.

The paper I'm holding feels alive. Vibrant. Mighty. As a journalist, I've always been a firm believer in the power of the pen, but still I've never experienced anything like this. Like Grandma Lucy — or maybe the Holy Spirit himself — is reaching into my soul, searching out the broken, fearful places. Breathing light into my darkness.

You are not forgotten. You are not abandoned. Jesus Christ, who suffered on that cross so that we might have life and have it more abundantly, is the gentle Shepherd who will carry his wounded sheep back into the safety of his pasture.

He will carry you too, Ian. He is carrying you now even when you can't feel his arms around you.

You are loved more than words can express. You are loved by the Creator of the heavens.

I don't just believe it. I know it. As certainly as I know that gravity exists or that the universe is more expansive than words could describe.

And now I entrust you into God's hands. May he heal you of all your illness, forgive you all your iniquities, and restore to you once more the joy of your salvation.

You are a beloved child of the King, and he has promised to take care of every single one of your needs.

I love you, Ian, and I look forward to one day rejoicing with you at the way the power of the holy blood of Jesus has set you free from everything that holds you captive.

She doesn't sign her letter. She doesn't say amen. I started crying after the first or second sentence, but now my tears have changed. They're not the hopeless tears of an ill inmate who might very well be on his deathbed reading his grandma's last farewell.

They're the tears of a redeemed soul, the prodigal son come home. These tears are the waters of my baptism, and the light that's burning in my chest is witness to the salvation and restoration that have taken place in my spirit.

I'm forgiven.

And no matter what happens from now on to my physical body, I know that I am free.

CHAPTER 50

Doc doesn't look very happy. Neither does Eric. *Malnutrition ... pneumonia ... systems shutting down ...*

I try to tell them both that my body's feeling stronger than it ever has, but there's a strange metallic taste in my mouth, and my tongue doesn't always seem to know how to form the words I want it to.

I wish they wouldn't worry so much about me, but Doc's probably going to lose his job and maybe his head if he lets me die. I'm Pyongyang's biggest bargaining chip, after all. Washington DC's not going to do any sort of bartering to secure the release of a corpse.

I should feel grateful I'm being kept alive, but mostly I'm just glad to be out of that prison camp. Any thoughts I had going in there about how it would be the opportunity to see footage no other American has seen vanished within the first few hours. After that it was only about survival, and even then my success at that was questionable at best.

Eric gives me a few letters each day. Some are from

family members like my Aunt Connie and my sister Alayna. Others are from strangers. I even have a few celebrities who've taken the time to write me.

"I have a friend here to visit you," Eric says one day, and I turn to the window hoping Rusty's returned. I still don't know what's become of that mangy mutt. I hope he's just found someplace warm to hunker down for the winter.

There's no dog, but a friendly smile towers above me. "Hello, American."

"Hee-Man."

His grin widens. "You remember me."

I don't tell him that for a while I worried he was a hallucination. I also don't tell him that the only way I found to curb my intense loneliness was to talk to him as if he'd been with me my entire prison stay. Instead I just say, "It's good to see you, man."

"You mean Hee-Man," he replies, and I'm happy.

We've just shared a joke.

"Hey, American?"

"What?"

"Do you know where Australians keep their money?"

I shake my head. True to form, Hee-Man's already laughing before he delivers the punchline. "In their pockets."

I pretend to laugh even though it hurts. It's far less painful than the loneliness I've experienced before Hee-Man's visit.

He sits on the corner of my bed and chats away easily. Apparently, his wife has recently delivered their third daughter. "That's why I could not come see you any sooner."

I want to give him a hard time, make him feel guilty for deserting me, but the truth is I'm so happy to see him I don't have the heart to tease.

"What is new with you?" he asks. "How is your health? Do you feel as bad as you look?"

"Probably. If I'd have known you were coming I would have freshened up." I have to explain the idiom, so the chance for humor has already passed. But that's okay. "Did you bring us any movies?" I try to make my voice sound lighthearted, but I'm actually serious.

He shakes his head. "Sorry, American. You will have to write a letter to your secretary and ask her to bring you some."

I try to explain to him that back home I'm a freelancer. I work for myself and don't have an office staff, but he's grinning at me like he's waiting for me to get the punchline of some great joke.

"No, American. I'm talking about the woman politician. Hamilton."

"The Secretary of State?" I glance over at Eric, expecting any news from the government to come from him. Apparently, he's in on the joke too and is smiling at us both.

"Secretary Hamilton is flying into Pyongyang," he tells me. "She'll be here in a week."

"What's she doing here?"

Hee-Man laughs as if I've just delivered the greatest punchline. "She is coming to take you home, American. So all you have to do is stay alive until then."

I'm not sure if this last part is also a joke or not, but I promise him I'll try.

CHAPTER 51

Hee-Man says he'll stay with me for the week. I expect he's probably anxious to go home to his newborn baby, but each time I mention this he just grins. "She cries too much. I sleep better in Pyongyang."

I remind myself that if I ever visit Hee-Man's hometown, it might be wise to avoid his wife. She probably hates me for stealing her husband. After a few days, I finally break down and tell Hee-Man how I spent my prison stay talking to him.

"Really?" Thankfully, he looks pleased instead of freaked out. "Tell me, did I come up with any good jokes while we were there together?"

He doesn't ask me about my time in prison camp, and other than an interview with Eric when I first got to the hospital, most people around here seem happy enough not to mention my time of forced labor.

I have a hard time believing that part of my past is really over, though. Each morning when Doc comes in, I brace myself for what I'm sure is coming. He's going to tell me I'm not sick anymore and that I have to go back to Camp 22 to finish out my sentence.

I've never studied the psychology of trauma that much, and to be honest, when I think about what the North Koreans who've been in places like Camp 22 for decades are going through, I'm ashamed to even use a word so strong. If what I went through was traumatic, there must be a word that even better portrays what they're suffering.

It's one of the few times that language eludes me.

I suppose it's possible to be traumatized and to know that others are suffering even worse fates than you, but it still doesn't seem right somehow. Just like it seems wrong that I'm here getting medical attention and IV nutrients while Camp 22 is filled with prisoners who are far more likely to see the inside of a torturer's chamber than a hospital room.

I think a lot about what Grandma Lucy and I spoke about so many years ago, her whole *with great power comes great responsibility* speech. I'm not about to turn into Spider-Man, return to Camp 22, and free everyone there after snatching their captors in my homespun webs. I figure the only way I'll ever get over this survivor's guilt I'm feeling is to promise myself to do even more to advocate for the North Koreans I left behind. Who else could speak up for them like that? I can only assume that the reason God spared my life is so that I can do even more to improve their lot.

Otherwise I'd be better off suffering there with them still.

I wonder how Grandma Lucy will take the news of my conversion. I wonder if she's already gotten the letter I passed on to Eric in response to her birthday note. Part of me's glad that she's on the other side of the world and not here to fawn over me and make a huge stinking deal about it all. Grandma Lucy's faith has and always will be loud, defiant, and brash. I'd prefer to go on living out my convictions in a much more quiet and subdued manner if it's all the same to her.

I wrote a letter to my girlfriend as well. I wonder if I can call her that again now that I'm saved. I wonder if she'll even recognize me once Hamilton comes and gets me out of here. Part of me is too ashamed to even think about her looking at me until I've regained some of my strength. But there's another part of me that says I should drop down on my knees the moment I'm with her again and beg her to spend the rest of her life with me.

This feeling of peace hasn't left me since I read Grandma Lucy's birthday note. Well, I take that back. When I'm all alone at night, even though I know Hee-Man's sleeping next door and there are nurses and guards within shouting distance, I still have to fight off the overwhelming sense of loneliness. Ironically, I slept better when I was in Camp 22 in that underground detainment center. I was so exhausted I dozed right off and didn't think about a thing until morning. Now I wake up from nightmares several times a night. I want to ask Hee-Man to bring his cot into my hospital room, but I'm too embarrassed.

It's early December now. I've spent the past few months convinced I'll be celebrating Christmas in North Korea, but now that Hee-Man's told me about Secretary Hamilton's trip to Pyongyang, I'm not sure. I don't want to get my hopes up too high, but it's possible, isn't it?

Anything's possible.

I've got to believe that.

But I've got to keep my head on too. If Secretary Hamilton's trip isn't successful, I still need to be ready to stick it out here for the long haul. I owe that to the North Koreans I suffered beside. I need to get healthy, stay healthy, and pray for my release.

It's funny. I imagine that many people in my situation would spend their time dreaming up ways to become better citizens, better Christians, better human beings once they're released. I feel like I should be doing the same, but looking back, I'd already committed the past several years of my life even before my imprisonment to promoting issues of social justice.

I want to keep doing the same.

The biggest difference is that by the time I get home — assuming Secretary Hamilton's trip is a success — I'll have an even bigger platform. I hate to think that I'm using my suffering to promote my own career, but I'm pretty sure that even as ambitious as I might be, my motives are far more altruistic than that.

At least I hope they are.

I'm also amused when I think about how strongly I opposed Christianity over the past decade or so. I was convinced that if I returned to the faith of my childhood, I'd automatically have to throw out everything I'd worked for, everything I knew, and become one of those Christians from Grandma Lucy's church who have nothing better to do with their time but fret and pout over who's sleeping with whom before they're married.

It's nice to know that my conversion — or maybe reconversion is a better term for it — didn't change who I fundamentally am.

I still feel like Ian. I'm still burdened by all the

injustice I see around the world. I still want to do something to make my mark on humanity and leave this globe a better place.

Somehow I wonder if I've been instinctively living out my Christian duty even during those years when I was convinced I was an atheist.

I don't tell Hee-Man about my conversion. It doesn't feel safe. I don't want to put him or his family in jeopardy, especially now that his wife has that brand-new baby of hers. I've never spent much time around newborns. I was too young when Alayna was born to remember her as an infant, and most of my friends are still single. The few who are in committed relationships are pretty adamantly opposed to having children at this stage in their lives. I wish Hee-Man had pictures of his new daughter. I'd like to see what she looks like. I wonder if there will be any way for the two of us to stay in touch once Secretary Hamilton brings me home.

I hear a scratching at the hospital window and turn automatically. I still haven't given up hopes of being reunited with Rusty, but it's just a hospital worker shoveling the snow outside. The IV in my arm burns, but other than that I feel comfortable enough.

I continue to stare out the window as wet snowflakes

float around in the winter breeze.

By this time next week, I could be a free man.

Maybe I'll be spending Christmas with Grandma Lucy after all.

Bigger miracles have happened before, haven't they?

After all, I'm still alive.

CHAPTER 52

It's hard to say if I'm improving or not, at least in terms of my health. As each passing day brings us closer to Secretary Hamilton's visit to Pyongyang, I feel stronger and more hopeful. I may not be the most intuitive soul in the world, but I've got a good feeling about this.

The problem is Doc doesn't seem to share my general optimism. According to his x-rays, my lungs are doing absolutely nothing to clear up this pneumonia, even with the heavy antibiotics he's been giving me. I don't worry. In just a few days, I'll be back in the States. My own medical coverage is the cheapest you can find on the marketplace, but I'm certain I'll have access to the best medical care political clout can buy. After all, think of how much information I can give DC about Pyongyang and North Korea.

They're not going to treat me as an expendable.

I don't want Doc to start worrying, but I think he must be prone to anxiety. Hee-Man's got to take off for a few days. Family duties. He doesn't say so, but I wouldn't be surprised if his wife's threatened to leave if he doesn't spend at least a little time with that newborn baby of his. I won't blame him for taking off to be with the ones he loves. Don't you think I'd do the same if I had the opportunity?

Days pass more slowly with Hee-Man gone. It's like that spring break between my third and fourth year of undergrad. I was all set to go to Florida with some friends of mine, but I got a nasty case of Empty Wallet Syndrome and ended up lounging around campus, sleeping in late, watching TV, and basically counting down the days until the semester started and all my friends got back to the dorms.

Except here there's no TV, and it's not some college party friends I'm waiting on. It's the Secretary of State herself. In the flesh. I've already agreed to put every single one of my political opinions aside when we meet. Who cares which administration she's working for or which president appointed her as long as she's come here to take me home?

One of the first things I'm going to do when I get my cell phone back is hop online and delete every nasty thing I've tweeted about the current political situation. One thing I've learned over the past few months is the world certainly doesn't need more divisiveness.

I know if I were as strong of a believer as Grandma Lucy,

I'd be spending this extra free time I have praying, singing hymns, all that stuff. But as thankful as I am to God for pulling me through these past few months and keeping me alive long enough for Secretary Hamilton to waltz in and rescue me, the truth is I just don't have the mental focus I need to spend much time in prayer. I hope the Lord's not disappointed in me.

Seeing as how he's such a God of grace and compassion, I'm pretty sure I can count on at least a little bit of leniency.

It's all going to take some getting used to, this whole life of faith thing. But first things first. I've got to get myself out of North Korea. Which means staying alive until Secretary Hamilton secures my release. I'm not trying to be melodramatic or anything, but Doc's a real pessimist when it comes to my case. The good thing is I know that he and all of Pyongyang want to keep me alive.

I don't need to worry.

I'm getting the best medical care the country has to offer. Which probably isn't saying a whole lot, but I know my chances are way better here than they would have been at the camp.

I'm going to be fine.

I just need to hold out for a few days longer.

CHAPTER 53

There's fussing around my room, and two men are bringing a camera in. I don't remember ordering a bedside interview.

My hospital room has never beheld such a crowd. There's Doc, Eric, and several faces I've never seen or only partially recognize. I have the vague impression I've been out of it for a while. Well, what do you expect when all I've got to do is lie around waiting for my superhero a.k.a. Secretary Hamilton to show up and fly me home?

Doc's forehead is beaded with sweat. Is he still worrying himself sick over me? *I'm fine* I want to tell him, but somehow I don't think he'll believe me.

For a moment, I worry that all this chaos has to do with my health, but I don't hurt anywhere. Come to think of it, I haven't experienced any kind of pain in a while. Which leaves me to wonder just how long I've been sleeping.

I glance around. I'm not sure if it's a good sign or not that my vision is this blurry. I don't think it's my eyes. I'm taking longer than normal to process what it is I'm looking at. Well, what do you expect when you've been lying in a hospital bed for this long? It probably has to do with all that emotional trauma I've gone through as well. Perfectly explainable. Perfectly normal.

I'm fine.

Out of nowhere, Hee-Man appears on the corner of my bed, sitting so close to me I could rest my head in his lap if I wanted. "How are you feeling, American?"

"I'm fine." Why does everyone look so worried? "How long have you been here?" I ask the question perfectly clearly, so I'm not sure why he's blinking at me like all of a sudden I'm speaking French.

"We are going to let you talk to your grandma," he tells me. "Would you like that?"

"Grandma Lucy?" I respond, only this time I hear myself and get the feeling my words aren't coming out quite right. Is she on the phone or something?

The camera's pointed at me, and someone places a laptop on the tray table by my bedside. For a minute, I get this feeling like it's time for me to deliver another confession, but I remember that aspect of my North Korean vacation's over. I'm hardly a prisoner anymore. I'm just a patient at the hospital waiting for my plane to come and take me to America.

Things will start making a lot better sense once I get home and get the medicine I really need. Kind as he is and as stressed out as he gets over my health, Doc's probably not the most capable physician I've ever met. I'd never tell him that though. He's doing everything in his power to keep me alive. If it weren't for him, I probably would have died already.

Hmm. Died. I wonder for a minute if that's what's going on, and for a brief second I start to panic. Has something happened to Grandma Lucy? Another heart attack? Is she on her deathbed and in a moment of humane diplomacy the North Koreans have allowed me to wish her a final farewell?

No. Grandma Lucy's the strongest woman alive. She'll never die. At least not like this.

So what's going on?

There's static on the screen, and then I'm blinking at my little white-haired granny.

"Hi." I try to smile, but my entire face burns.

"Hello, precious. Are you feeling well?"

I think I am, but seeing Doc's worried face and sensing the fear in my friend Hee-Man have made me a little less certain. And why did my body pick now of all times to start leaking tears?

She holds her hand up to the screen until all I can see is

her palm. She starts praying for me, and I'm certain she's made a mistake. Doesn't she know how religion is opposed here? She can't go doing stuff like this or they'll sever the connection.

Except they don't.

I can't hear the words she's saying. Actually, that's not quite right. I hear them, but I can't piece them together into coherent meaning. All I know is that she's praying for me as passionately as anyone ever has in my entire life. Eric's standing off to the side looking stoic, Doc's still sweating up a storm, and Hee-Man's holding my hand like I'm a lost little orphan he's trying to comfort.

I still don't quite know what's going on until my brain finally manages to latch on to something Grandma Lucy says. "… his homecoming be peaceful and free of pain." I get the sense she's not talking about my flight back to the States with Secretary Hamilton either. Finally it all makes sense. The big rush to get a camera in here. Doc's anxiety. Hee-Man's gentle cries.

I'm dying.

CHAPTER 54

I slip in and out of consciousness until I lose all track of time. When I open my eyes, I have no idea if it's been two minutes or two days since the last time I was awake.

Sometimes Hee-Man's here, and sometimes he's not. I get the feeling that weeks have passed, months even, but I know that can't be the case.

Doc looks less nervous now and more resigned. I'm not sure that's a good thing when you're talking about the man charged with keeping you from death. But I'm so tired I hardly care. I want to tell him he's done a good job. He's done all he can. I don't even hurt anywhere. He doesn't have to be afraid for me.

But talking takes too much effort, and after a minute I always fall back to sleep anyway. It's nice. Peaceful. Painless.

Just like Grandma Lucy prayed that it would be.

I remind myself to thank her once we're reunited in heaven.

CHAPTER 55

"Are you awake, American?"

I blink my eyes open. It's Hee-Man. No matter how tired I am, I always do my best to smile when he's around. I know he doesn't have to be here. He could be back home with his family. It's nice of him to keep me company like this. Nice of him to care so much.

"Merry Christmas," he says. The words fly at me through a dense fog. He's smiling and holding up a flash drive. "I got you a present."

It doesn't make sense. "Christmas?"

He nods. "You have been asleep for a while."

Maybe Christmas comes earlier in Pyongyang. That's one way of explaining it.

"Do you feel strong enough for me to help you sit up?" Hee-Man asks, but my brain's still fixating on Christmas.

What about Secretary Hamilton's visit?

What about going home?

"What day is it?" I mumble, just like Ebenezer

256

Scrooge waking up, trying to figure out everything he missed.

"Christmas," Hee-Man answers readily.

I feel the start of a pounding headache. I wince. "It can't be."

"December 25th," Hee-Man recites proudly. "Christmas Day."

"What about the Secretary?"

His smile fades. "It did not work this time, American. But do not worry. Your people are still working to get you home."

I can't understand his words. *It did not work*? That's what you say when you spend ten bucks on a cheap trinket at the toy store and it breaks half a day later.

"She's supposed to take me home," I croak.

Hee-Man sighs loudly. "Not this time, I am afraid. But cheer up. It is Christmas, and Doc says your fever has finally come down. You are getting better."

I can't figure out how I can be getting better when I've spent what must have been a couple weeks in painless delirium, and now I'm awake with the most piercing headache a human being can endure without passing out.

"Do you want to watch your present?" Hee-Man's still holding up the flash drive.

"What is it?"

"A Christmas movie."

"Well, which one?" I've never cared for cheesy Christmas flicks, but maybe some nostalgia will do me good. Help me figure out what's going on with my body and mind, help me understand what Hee-Man means when he says it's December 25th but I'm still not home.

"*Die Hard*," Hee-Man answers. "With the same actor from the outer space one." I wonder if my friend knows how many Americans fight about whether *Die Hard* classifies as a Christmas movie or not. As far as I'm concerned, Hee-Man's assumption has ended all debate. If a North Korean who doesn't even celebrate Christmas and is outlawed from watching foreign films can see it for what it really is, that settles the argument once and for all in my humble opinion.

I'd usually be up for something like this, but I simply can't. I've seen too much violence already to stomach something like this.

"Maybe later," I tell Hee-Man and look away so I don't have to see the disappointment in his face. My head throbs. Holiday or no holiday, he should have never woken me up.

I roll toward the window. It's been so long since I've seen Rusty I don't even check outside anymore.

Hee-Man asks if I'm hungry, says he convinced the

hospital staff to cook me something special. I wonder how long it's been since I've actually eaten. If I've survived this long on nothing but my IV fluids, I'm sure missing one more meal isn't going to hurt.

"Right now, I think I want to get a little more sleep."

CHAPTER 56

I can't be entirely certain, but I think I'm floating, and even though I know my brain hasn't been quite as clear as I'd like it to be for this past little stretch, I realize enough to know that there are two potential scenarios going on. Either I'm dreaming, or I'm already dead. Both possibilities seem just as likely, although the fact that I'm experiencing absolutely no pain at the moment is making me lean towards the latter.

Poor Grandma Lucy. She's going to be heartbroken.

No sooner do I have the thought than I'm sitting in her prayer room, staring at her as she rocks in her prayer chair and waiting patiently for her to open her eyes. "Oh, hello, Ian. How nice to see you."

Somewhere in the back of my head is the thought that she should be a bit more surprised to find me here, but I don't dwell on this for very long.

"How are you, Grandma?"

She smiles. "I'm starting to feel my age these days."

I roll my eyes. "Tell me about it."

She doesn't seem to have heard me, or at least she doesn't respond directly. "Still, there's lots to be thankful for," she continues, "isn't there?"

I nod my head, and we sit there staring at one another comfortably. She rocks her chair gently back and forth, and each time she comes forward her knees press against mine.

"How are things in Pyongyang?" she finally asks.

"Not bad. Not bad at all." I hear a dog bark and immediately think about Rusty before I remember that I'm sitting at my grandma's house in a little town in Washington.

Sort of.

"Is Doc still worried about you?"

I nod. "He's a good guy. He is doing all he can, but it's a lot of pressure on him. He'll be in pretty big trouble if something happens to me, and he knows it."

"So what happens now?" Grandma Lucy asks, as if I have any control or say in the matter.

"Not sure." I'm surprised at how casually she's talking about things, as if she does this every single day. "Hamilton's trip didn't work." I'm using the same language Hee-man did.

Grandma Lucy nods. This is obviously no surprise to her. "Diplomacy takes time," she sagely remarks.

I decide to confess something. "To be honest, I'm not sure how much time I have left."

She continues nodding at me as she rocks gently back and forth. The rhythm is lulling, almost hypnotic. "So what do you think you're going to do?"

"I still haven't decided." I let out a sigh. "I guess that's why I came here to have this little chat with you." It's all news to me, but my answer makes sense, at least in the mental state that I'm in.

"Have you prayed about it? Have you asked what God wants you to do?"

I shrugged. "I'm not as good at praying as you are. Still not convinced I'm doing it right."

Now it's her turn to shrug. "All you got to do is open your mouth and start talking."

"I know that. But some people are better talkers than others."

She signs for me to wait a minute before she raises her eyes to mine. "Which would you choose, Ian?" I know this is the question we've been skirting around, and I know exactly what she means. I never would have guessed that a choice like this would be left up to me.

"If you come here," she says, "you can resume your work. Finish that documentary. You'll be advancing God's kingdom by living to tell your story."

I nod. I've already thought through all the pros and cons.

"If you go home," she says, "you will be healed. No more pain, no more nightmares, no more trauma."

I want to say something smart-alecky like *ay, there's the rub*, but for some reason, I remain quiet and contemplative.

"You know you're the only one who can make this choice."

I sense the heaviness of disappointment descend on me. I was afraid she would say something like that.

"It would be so much easier if you told me what to do," I admit.

She smiles at me softly. "Maybe you should listen to your friend. What's Hee-man think about it?"

I'm about to tell her that Hee-man and I can't talk about things as directly she and I are doing right now, but she floats away from me, still smiling peacefully, and the throbbing pain in my head, my chest, my entire body is back.

"Please heal him," someone is whispering in my ear.

Hee-Man? Is that you? I hallucinated about my friend so many times when I was in prison camp that I can't judge whether this is real or not.

Says the man who was just now having a conversation

with his grandmother who lives on the other side of the world, chatting peacefully about whether it's time to die or not.

"Please strengthen him and deliver him from his illness," Hee-Man says, and I realize that he's praying for me. What was it that Grandma Lucy told me about listening to my friend?

"Heal him in the name of Jesus."

I want to grin as if I've caught Hee-Man doing something naughty. *I knew you were a Christian*, I want to say, but it's too dangerous. I don't want to get him in trouble, not when he has a family and a new baby to support. Not when he's been so kind to me. And thinking back for a moment to our standoffs in that little hotel room before we even came to Pyongyang. I want to chuckle when I remember the confession I wrote him about how I worked for Nick Fury and the Avengers.

Instead, I force my eyes open. It's like wading upstream through a river of syrup to force his image into focus. My body is on fire. Every bone aches, and the stinging in my chest makes it so that I can only move air a milliliter at a time. But still, there's something comforting about seeing my friend here at my bedside.

"Hi," I manage to croak out.

He lets out his breath. I've never seen him look so relieved. "You are awake."

"Yeah, there's only so much beauty sleep a handsome guy like me needs."

Hee-Man blinks at me.

"It's a joke," I tell him. For a moment, I think about letting him know that I heard his prayer. I think about how nice it would be for us both to be able to acknowledge the fact that we're now praying to the same God, but something holds me back. It's still too dangerous.

"How long have I been asleep?" I ask.

"It is the middle of January," he tells me.

I do what I can to make my voice sound angry. "Why didn't you wake me up sooner?"

He-man gives me a forlorn look. "Because you are so sick. We all thought you were about to die."

I shake my head and scold him. "That's really no excuse." I can't stand the sad expression on his face, so I soften my voice. "It's a joke," I tell him.

He gives me a smile that is far from convincing but is nevertheless filled with warmth and sympathy.

"I am glad you are feeling better," he says.

"Yeah," I reply. "Thanks for waking me up."

CHAPTER 57

Over the next few days, I'm in constant pain, certain I've made a terrible mistake. Sometimes when I fall asleep, I secretly hope for another chance to chat with Grandma Lucy in her prayer room to let her know I've changed my mind. I'd rather cash in my ticket to heaven, but it seems that the choice to survive is no longer mine to make.

Hee-man never leaves my side. I tell him that baby of his must have a really bad disposition if he finds my company more bearable than hers, but I'm not sure he gets the joke.

Everyone hovers over me — Doc, the Swedish ambassador. I haven't been outside in months, but one morning I'm woken up by a familiar sound.

Ruff.

I can't turn my head fast enough. There at the window, his paws trying to dig through the glass to get to me, is the ugliest, most mangy dog I've ever seen.

266

"Where have you been, boy?" I ask even though my voice is so weak I can scarcely hear myself. I just have to put my trust in everything I've been told about a dog's supersensitive ears.

He cocks his head to the side, a question in his eyes. *Aren't you coming out to play?* I'm sure that's what he's asking me.

"I don't think they'll let me outside yet." I'm still so loopy, whether from the drugs or my illness. I'm not even sure if I'm talking to him out loud or just in my mind. I make him a promise that I'll try to regain some strength so we can play. Even through the foggy window, I can tell his hair is matted and in need of a good combing.

"You seem to be getting stronger," Doc tells me after listening to my chest later that day. "I think the medicine's finally starting to work."

I glance toward the window. Given my mental state, I'm a little worried I didn't see Rusty after all. My mind may have just made that all up in my feverish delirium, but my mutt is still there.

"Should we bring him inside?" Doc asks. I'm so used to being trapped in my own mind it takes me a while to comprehend what he's saying. Doc smiles and makes his way to the door. "It's freezing out there. Why don't we bring him in to warm up a little?"

This is a more joyous feeling than any Christmas or birthday I've ever had. The minute Doc leads him into my room, Rusty jumps onto my bed, but he must have been gifted with some sort of super canine sense that tells him I'm weak and that he needs to be careful with me.

For a joyous eternity, he's done nothing but whine and lick my face. His breath is just as foul as I remember, but I don't mind his canine baptism. I scratch his ears, rub his belly, wrap my arms around him and soak in his warmth and his strength. Any minute, I'm certain a hospital worker will come in and take my friend away, but it's well after sunset before I see Doc again. He's carrying a large blanket and lays it down between the hospital bed and my window. Rusty seems to understand what it's for even before I do, and he hops down, spinning himself in three full circles before finally settling down on his new bed.

I'm pretty sure that having a dog in my hospital room is a bad idea from a sanitation standpoint, but I already feel so much stronger after cuddling him that I know Rusty's presence is going to be critical for my recovery.

I have no idea what day it is. I have no idea how much time has passed since I came so close to death, but I'm certain of one thing. I'm not going to die in this hospital room, and I'm not going to spend the rest of my life in North Korea either. Somehow, someway, I'm going to make it. I'm getting out of here.

And I'm taking my dog with me.

CHAPTER 58

I sit comfortably across from Grandma Lucy in her rocking chair. She and I have met so many times like this in my dreams I don't even wait to be invited anymore before taking my seat.

"How are you today, Ian?"

I let out my breath. "Oh, pretty good. How about yourself?"

Grandma Lucy stares out her window. "Not bad. Not bad at all. I get forgetful sometimes. I think it has Connie worried."

"Aunt Connie's always going to worry about you," I tell her.

This makes Grandma Lucy smile. "So she is. And what about you? I hear the Secretary of State is scheduled to make another visit to your neck of the woods."

"Yeah, but how did you know about that? Eric said they're keeping the trip secret."

Grandma Lucy taps the leather Bible on her lap. "I have

my ways of finding these things out."

I'm sure she does.

"So, are you excited to be coming home?" she asks.

It's strange talking like this, like my return to the US is assured. In spite of how encouraged Eric is about this upcoming visit, he's always reminding me not to get my hopes raised too high. "Don't forget what happened last time," he keeps saying.

But somehow I'm not worried. My health has improved. I can sit up in bed without getting too exhausted. I'm staying awake for more than five or ten minutes at a time, and I've even managed to make myself coherent when I'm chatting with Hee-Man.

"There's only two things I'm going to miss here," I admit.

Grandma Lucy smiles. She already knows, which really shouldn't surprise me seeing as how this is my dream and we're in my subconscious.

"Hee-Man," she states. "And your dog."

I nod.

"You know they won't really let you take a mangy mutt on a government plane all the way to Washington, don't you?"

"Yeah. But I can't stand the thought of just leaving him

here." When I'm gone, who's going to scratch Rusty behind his ears or tickle him on the tummy or comb out the matts he'll inevitably get in his fur?

"You know there's a simple solution," Grandma Lucy tells me.

I sigh. "You're probably right."

"It'll be the best for everyone involved."

"I know."

"You better go now," Grandma Lucy tells me. "Secretary Hamilton will be there any minute." I don't ask her how she knows this, but I suspect it's true.

"So I'll see you soon?" I ask.

She smiles while rocking back and forth in her chair. "You know right where I'll be."

CHAPTER 59

Secretary Hamilton is just as unsmiling and formidable as she appears whenever I see her on the news. There's very little softness or gentleness in her voice. "Your health is improving." I have a hard time figuring out if she's asking me to confirm this or telling me what she believes is true.

Doc bustles to her side, rattling off my multiple diagnoses and his expectation that with continued medical supervision I'll make a full recovery.

I keep my attention divided between my two best friends. Rusty's lying on his side, his head cocked. Hee-Man is sitting at the foot of my bed. He doesn't seem to have an official reason to be here anymore now that I've been released back into American custody, but nobody has yet found the heart to ask him to leave. I'm glad.

After all these months, I'm actually going home.

It doesn't feel real, but then again, I've never before been incarcerated for months, nursed back to health from the point of death, and then visited by a famous American politician who traveled across the globe to fly me home.

Rusty puts his paws up on my bed and whines. I've asked Hamilton multiple times if I can bring him with me. She can't understand why I care so much about this ugly stray. I should be ecstatic. Tonight I'm getting on a plane to fly out of Pyongyang. I should be dancing a jig, not sitting here moping and whining about a dog. At least that's what Hamilton thinks. She doesn't understand how much of my healing I owe to this mutt.

To this mutt and to Hee-Man's prayers for me.

I still haven't let on that I know his secret. That I know he prays. That I know he's a believer. I'm going to respect his privacy and wait for the day when North Korea is free and I can visit him at his home and he can take me to his church.

That's the hope I'm holding onto. That's what makes it bearable to tell Hee-Man goodbye.

But Rusty is already old. I'm no veterinarian, but I can tell he's got pain in his hips. The hair around his muzzle is gray, and I'm sure he's far past his prime. Once I get on the plane with Secretary Hamilton, I'll never see him again.

I pat the bed, and Rusty hops up beside me. His usual energy and enthusiasm are gone. I wonder how much he understands. If he realizes this is goodbye.

I bury my head against his forehead. I don't care if Hamilton thinks I'm sentimental. "You take care of yourself," I croak.

Hee-Man comes over to me next. Who would have thought that leaving North Korea would be this excruciating? I should be jumping up and down in the streets for joy, except I don't have the physical strength, and I'm too heavy-hearted.

Hee-Man puts his hand on Rusty's head. "I'll make sure to take good care of him. My daughters are already bursting from excitement to meet him."

At least I know that Rusty will be loved. It's all that I can do.

"One more thing." Hee-Man reaches into his pocket and pulls out a hard drive.

"What's this?"

"A late Christmas present."

I eye him suspiciously.

"*Die Hard*," he tells me. I don't have the heart to tell him that in the States I could download *Die Hard* or stream it on any device I own.

"Thank you." I hope he knows my gratitude extends toward far more than giving me a bootlegged movie and adopting my dog.

Eric Swensson steps up to shake my hand. "Good luck back in the US."

I thank him for everything he's done to help me. None of his advocacy would technically fall under his job description as the Swedish ambassador. It's as if he's volunteered all these hours to secure my release.

Doc is rattling off instructions, presumably for my care, but Hee-Man isn't translating and Secretary Hamilton isn't listening. "Are you ready to go?" she asks me.

I take a deep breath. I can walk the length of my room and back when I'm gifted with a burst of energy, but that's about all I can expect of myself at the moment.

Fortunately, Hee-Man has already found a wheelchair for me. "Here you go, American."

I smile at him. "You just want one last chance to push me around, don't you?" I ask.

He smiles at me. "You are making a joke."

"Yes, I am."

"It is funny, American. Very funny."

CHAPTER 60

My return to the States is nothing like what I would have expected. The US government managed to keep Secretary Hamilton's trip a secret. The only people who meet us when we land near D.C. are some Feds in suits. They don't want me talking to the media until I've been debriefed, and the American physician who met Hamilton and me in Hamburg, Germany, doesn't want me to be debriefed until I've regained my strength.

It's not until I'm in the American hospital that I realize how truly sick I am. The doctor assigned to me shows me the x-rays, tells me how many bacterial pockets have set up residence in my lungs, and explains the lab reports that convey how close all my systems came to shutting down completely. I always knew I was sick, but it's sobering to have the scientific facts explained to me in English.

My days are a blur of physical therapy and government interviews, and finally I'm declared well enough to fly to Seattle to complete my recovery closer to family. I'll still be in the hospital for a while, but I'll be near Grandma Lucy and out of government custody.

I don't have the heart to tell all these Feds that I was made to feel more welcomed in North Korea than I was in their care.

By the time I reach Seattle, the news outlets have picked up my story. Grandma Lucy tells me I have enough mail to fit into a fifty-pound potato sack. She and Aunt Connie will be meet me at the hospital. I'm another step closer to home.

I can hardly wait. I've got one more debriefing interview to get through this afternoon, then the doctor's escorting me to Seattle.

"You're a lucky man, Ian," he tells me when he comes in. I've lost track of how many people have told me this, and I've started to wonder how helpful it really is. Why is it that I'm here in America, being treated by the finest doctors, while thousands of other men and women and even children are laboring in Camp 22 with no hope of reprieve or diplomatic intervention?

Survivor's guilt is a real thing. It's even more poignant than the guilt I've carried around for being a straight white male in an Anglocentric world because now I've seen what happens behind the barbed wire fence. I know the despair those prisoners are experiencing right now. And who is advocating for them?

One of the women from my debriefing team comes in. I forget her title. I've met far too many bureaucrats over the last few days to remember them all.

"Looks like your paperwork for your transfer to Seattle has checked out," she says as if she's a detective who has just confirmed my alibi.

I don't say anything to this. She's the third person in the last half hour to come in and tell me so.

The doctor's writing a few things on his chart, and the woman pulls out her cell. "We found something I want you to have a look at. Maybe you can explain it to me."

She holds the screen out in front of me, and even now that the antibiotics have nearly kicked the last of this pneumonia, my breath catches. Is that what I think it is?

I don't answer her. I have too many questions of my own. How she got it. Where she found it.

Her expression softens just a little. "This was on the flash drive we found with your things."

"Flash drive?" I try to remember. I haven't used flash drives since my undergrad days.

"Yes. It contained this photo and a pirated copy of *Die Hard*."

"Oh." I stare at the dirt-stained boy in the screen. I'm sorry I didn't find a way to help him directly when I was in his homeland. I'm sorry that he got in trouble with the police because of me. I can only hope that what Hee-Man told me is true and the factory where he was sent to work provided him with food and lodging and got him off of the streets.

"I take it you recognize this photo," the agent tells me, and I nod. I'm glad she doesn't force me to say anything. I don't know if it's my health or the medicine or all the stress I've been under, but I feel ready to break with the slightest provocation, to start crying and crumble beneath a pile of sadness and regret and fear I haven't even been able to put into words. The doctor's assured me that one of the best trauma psychologists will be waiting to speak with me in Seattle, but I'm starting to wonder if any amount of therapy can heal me from what I've endured.

Which again leads me to my overwhelming sense of guilt. Who will pay for the prisoners at Camp 22 to sit down and talk to a licensed therapist? What makes me so special that I should be granted this privilege when they're still starving and enslaved?

It's Grandma Lucy's words again that ring in my ears. *People will listen to you and accept you as an authority. To him who has been given much, much will be demanded.*

I'll do no good to anyone if I stay where I am. I need to heal. I need to recover. Then I can talk about what I went through, and after that maybe something will change.

I don't know what. I don't know how. I only know that the suffering others are enduring around the world needs to be brought to light before any improvements can be made. And somehow, for some reason I'll never understand, I've been chosen to deliver this message. It won't be easy. I'd much rather forget about everything I went through and vow to never think about the Korean peninsula again.

But I can't.

One day all injustice will be made right. I believe it. I've got to believe it. Otherwise life would be too depressing. It would have been better for me to have died in Pyongyang, forgotten and alone.

But I didn't die in Pyongyang. Jesus set me free. And he told me that from him who's been given much, much will be demanded. This is my calling. This is my burden.

"I have the flash drive here." The agent holds it out to me. "What would you like me to do with it?"

I'm ashamed at how recently I saw this photograph and thought of nothing but prizes and glory. I'm surprised at how thoroughly I've changed.

I take the flash drive and hold it in my palm. It feels solid in my hand, and my body doesn't shake. "I'll take that," I tell her.

I know just what to do with it too.

CHAPTER 61

It's not until I hear my aunt's voice coming down the hospital hallway that I start to feel nervous. I've settled into my room in Seattle, and the doctors are finally letting her and Grandma Lucy in.

They've been warned, haven't they? They know how much weight I've lost, how weak I am?

It's funny how many times I've imagined this reunion. In my mind, it was always on a tarmac surrounded by the media, not in a hospital room guarded by Feds, but this is the dream that sustained me for the seven months I spent in North Korea. Being with my family again. Being able to wish Grandma Lucy the happy birthday she deserves.

Except now I'm scared.

What if they don't recognize me? Even worse, what if they think I'm so damaged they whisper and tiptoe and second-guess everything they say? It's too late for being afraid. The door opens.

"Ian." Aunt Connie rushes forward and nearly crushes my

lungs with her hug. This is good. It means she's not afraid of me. It hurts like the dickens, but it's still better for my pride than if she'd been too timid.

And then she steps aside, and I see my grandma, wearing those pants that button up inches above her belly button, that polyester blouse with a collar as billowy as a kite. She looks smaller than I remember. Has she lost weight too?

She takes a step toward me. "Hello, Ian."

"It's good to see you, Grandma."

She takes my hand in hers. There's no bone-crushing hug, no profuse show of tears like Aunt Connie's in the corner. Grandma Lucy stares at me intently. "I knew you'd make it home. I just knew it."

"Thank you," I tell her. "For everything."

One of my guards is thoughtful enough to pull up a chair so Grandma Lucy can sit. Watching the love and joy in her eyes, I'm ashamed that I was worried about her seeing me like this.

"You've been eating well since you've been released?" she asks.

I nod. It wasn't until coming back to the States that I realized my taste buds had completely shut down. I can only taste the most basic of flavors. Salty. Sweet. But the trauma psychologist doesn't seem too surprised, and the fact that my appetite's picking up has made everyone pleased.

"Your Aunt Connie made you some cinnamon rolls." Grandma Lucy takes the handbag from Connie and pulls out two pastries wrapped in plastic. Just as I envisioned in my dreams, they're bigger than my head.

I don't know what to say. I desperately want to nap, but I have to make myself stay awake.

Grandma Lucy seems happy just to sit here and watch me, so I sink my head back in my pillow and rest my eyes. I'm not trying to be rude. I hope she knows how glad I am she's here. I hope she knows how happy I am to see her.

But my eyelids are so heavy. And this bed is so warm and comfortable ...

"Poor darling. Is he asleep?" I hear Aunt Connie ask.

I smile to myself, picturing the expressions on Hee-Man's daughters' faces when he introduces Rusty to them for the first time.

"He's had a long journey," Grandma Lucy declares. "A journey that is far from over."

I take in a deep breath, grateful as I feel my recovering lungs expanding with air. I'm looking down over Camp 22 like a bird flying free above the prison. I see the dorms and the outhouses where I had to haul waste. The school where I was paraded in front of the class like an animal. The detainment center where I spent my tenure underground.

When I wake up, I know these memories will bring sorrow, fear, and that ever-persistent sense of guilt. I know that these memories might haunt me forever.

But right now, as I soar high above the barbed wire fence that held me prisoner, I see hope where before there was only despair. Light strong enough to penetrate even the most pervasive darkness.

I don't know how, and I don't know when, but I know that one day these prison gates will fall. The watchtowers will crumble, and in their place flowers will grow. The detainment center where countless prisoners are now held in fear will be torn down, along with the dorms and factories where so many worked and lived in despair.

The land itself will be purged, and in place of this prison, symbols of culture and freedom will emerge. Libraries. Museums. Churches.

I don't know how, and I don't know when, but I believe that one day the Lord will allow me to return to the land of my captivity, and I'll stand here on this same ground, now made hallowed. And there, along with the tens of thousands of believers like my friend Hee-Man who is forced to live out his faith in secret, I will raise my hands and praise the God who truly is sovereign over every nation.

The God who brings freedom to the captives and release from darkness for the prisoners.

The God who can redeem even the most oppressive evils and work them together for his good and glorious purposes.

"Maybe we should step out and let him rest," I hear Aunt Connie say, but Grandma Lucy doesn't respond. She's resting her forehead on my hospital pillow, gripping my hand in hers, and lifting her prayers of thanks and petition to the God who delivered me out of all my fears and brought me back to this land of freedom and hope.

The God who rescued me out of North Korea.

A NOTE FROM THE AUTHOR

I hope you enjoyed *Out of North Korea*. Interestingly, even though he's not always mentioned by name, Ian shows up in many of my other novels. You might be especially interested in *The Beloved Daughter*, a story of Christian persecution set in Camp 22, and *Flower Swallow*, which is about the little boy in Ian's photograph.

If you enjoy suspense, you might also like to check out the Kennedy Stern Christian suspense series. Ian makes an appearance (sometimes named and sometimes not) in each book of this series as well.

A huge thank you (as always) to my husband, my editing team, and those who pray these novels into existence. Another huge thank you (as always) to everyone who reads these books. Your enthusiasm is so encouraging to me.

If you'd like more compelling Christian fiction, you can receive three full-length novels when you join the Alana Terry Readers' Club at www.alanaterry.com.

Made in the USA
Middletown, DE
16 July 2020